ROBERT

THE MCCLAINS BOOK 2

KIRSTEN OSBOURNE

UNLIMITED DREAMS

CHAPTER ONE

ENGLAND, 1135

Matilda looked around her nervously. It was her first day of work at the Lain Castle. She had grown up in the shadow of the castle, and her parents were serfs who worked the land owned by the Lain family. She had been chosen to be the new maid at the castle, which would be hard work but would be much easier than working the land as her parents and their parents had done.

She walked toward the castle with her mother at her side.

"Ignore anything odd you see. The family is

known for their strange ways. Just keep out of trouble, do what you are told, and you will be fine."

Matilda nodded, overwhelmed by the sight of the castle so close. She was used to seeing it off in the distance. She had lived in the shadow of the castle her entire life. "I will be home on Sunday," she said softly.

"Aye, you will. You were promised you would have every Sunday off, and you will spend them with your parents as you should." Her mother clutched her arm. "And if anything bad happens, you come right home to me."

Matilda looked at her mother. "Bad? The Lains are known for their love of the serfs. They are not bad people."

"That is true, but they do still have a son living at home. If you catch his eye, he might be interested in you doing more than emptying his chamber pot. Do not let him do more. You are a pretty girl, Mattie. I do not want to think about you being hurt."

Matilda nodded. "Aye, Mother." She leaned down and hugged her mother tightly. She was the only one of eight children who had survived to be old enough to work for someone. She knew her mother would worry if she could not see her every day. "I will be there early Sunday morning. Or if they will let me, I will come back Saturday night when my chores are finished." She hated the idea of her mother worrying about her, but their family needed the coins she would earn for working for the Lains.

"You are a good girl, Mattie. I hope this job blesses you beyond your wildest dreams." With those words, her mother turned away, leaving her to go to the big, bustling castle alone.

Matilda took a deep breath, squared her shoulders, and walked the short distance left to the castle. When she reached the moat, she walked across the bridge that put her in the castle's land. This was the area where the lord's army practiced for war and where the family would always be.

She kept walking and went to the back entrance, next to the kitchens. It was the servant's entrance, and she felt like an interloper. Pounding on the door, she waited, and a woman came to the door, looking down at her. "You the new maid?"

Matilda nodded. "Aye. I am to start today."

The older woman, who had gray hair and four black teeth, studied her for a moment. "You are too pretty to be an upstairs maid. We will put you in charge of dusting the furniture and sweeping the downstairs. It is about time Mary was promoted to be the upstairs maid anyway." She opened the door wider. "Come in! Come in! What are you waiting for?"

Matilda stepped over the threshold, forcing herself not to make the sign of the cross over her chest. The stories of this family made her very nervous. "I brought an extra dress with me," she said, holding up the bundle of clothes in her hand.

"Mary!" the woman called. "I need you to take this girl to her room. She is going to be moving into Agnes's old room."

Mary nodded and took Matilda by the arm, taking her up a steep staircase behind the kitchen. "This is where all the castle help stays, up here in this hallway. Agnes just married one of the local serfs, so she moved to his home. What's your name anyway?"

Matilda noted that Mary was only a couple of years older than she was, but she had obviously been working in the castle for a while. At eighteen, Matilda had never even dreamed that she would be living in a castle. She felt a bit like a fairy princess. "I am Matilda, but my family calls me Mattie. Have you worked here long?"

"Oh, aye. I have been here four years, and I know all the peculiarities of this family. You will learn them, too, but you cannot tell anything you see." Mary opened a door of a tiny room that had just enough space for a bed. There was a single window looking out over the courtyard where the soldiers trained.

Matilda looked around, her eyes wide. She had not ever imagined she would live in such luxury. "You mean I do not have to share?" Never in her life had she not shared a room with her parents. Their entire home could have fit in two rooms this size.

"Nah. Not here. The Lains take good care of those who work for them." Mary grinned. "Put your things away, and I will take you back down to Alice. She is the housekeeper, and she makes sure we all do what we are told and that the castle is always ready for guests."

"Do they have many guests?" Matilda asked, putting her extra dress into a chest at the foot of the bed. It was the only furniture in the room, but it was so much more than she had ever had before. She had been told servants usually slept in the great hall on rushes. Here . . . well, this was like living in a fantasy world.

"Not too many. Mainly just their grown sons coming back for visits with their families. There is only one son left here at the house, and that is Robert. He will be the one to inherit someday."

Matilda frowned, standing up to follow Mary back out of the room. "I thought Robert was the youngest son. Do not the oldest sons always inherit?" That was what she had always thought the nobility did. Had she been wrong?

"Not in this family. There is always something special about the seventh son, so he will be the one to inherit. I am not sure I quite understand it myself, but this place is different than any other in all of England. All of the world!"

As she followed to the bottom of the stairs and back to the kitchen, Matilda thought about Mary's words. The family was different. That could be good or bad. She just hoped it ended up being a good thing.

When she got to the bottom of the stairs, the woman Mary had called Alice was waiting for her. "For today, I want you to follow Mary around, and she will show you exactly what needs to be done."

Matilda nodded. "Aye."

Mary led the way out of the kitchen to the main floor of the house. "The work is simple and not too hard. You will need to dust and sweep and mop the downstairs every day. If there is something special Lady Lina wants, she will let you know, and you will do it. Very easy."

Mary handed Matilda a rag, and the two of them set to work dusting the main sitting room there on the first floor. Matilda could not help but notice what a nice space it was with solid oak furniture. She spotted a book and ran her hand over the cover. She had been taught to read by her local priest, who was something of a rebel. He believed women should be allowed to read the same as men were.

"You may read it if you would like," a soft voice said from the doorway.

Matilda jumped and shook her head. "Oh no, it would not be right!"

"I do not know why not." The woman who belonged to the voice stepped into the room. She had blond hair, and her smile was sweet. "I am Lady Lina. And you are?"

"Matilda, milady." Matilda looked down, afraid she would offend the lady of the castle by meeting her eyes.

"It is her first day," Mary said from across the room. "She is a little nervous."

Lady Lina shook her head. "No need to be nervous. I am sure you will do a wonderful job, and I would like for you to read the book. I could see by the look in your eyes that you wanted to."

"It does not bother you that I can read?" Matilda asked, surprised.

"Not at all. I read as well." It was a skill uncommon of women in the year of 1135, but the lady of the house was obviously not ashamed of being able to do it.

"You do?"

"Aye, my mother taught me when I was a young

girl. In this castle, we encourage women to learn every skill they can, so they can be just as strong as men, though in different ways."

Matilda smiled, feeling as if a warmth had spread through her from her toes. "I would be proud to borrow it then, milady."

"Wonderful! Welcome to the family, Matilda." Lady Lina swept out of the room, obviously intent on making someone else happy.

Matilda turned and looked at Mary. "She is so nice. Surely she is not the mistress here."

"Oh, but she is. And she is the family member we will have the most contact with here in the castle. Lady Lina treats everyone as if she is a family member, and she even has skills with herbs and potions to heal people." Mary shrugged. "Many people are afraid of the family, but I promise you there is not a better family to be found in all of England. If she had thought you could not read and wanted to, why she would have taught you herself."

"Really? How does her lord feel about this?" Matilda was truly surprised to hear that a woman of the nobility was so kind to others.

"Really. He lets her do what she wishes for the most part. He is obviously a man who knows that women need to be able to exercise their own wills.

Lord Alex is a wonderful man." Mary went back to dusting a chest in one corner of the room.

"I heard there was a son left at home, and he was well . . . odd." Matilda knew she should not bring it up, but she would be nervous until she understood exactly what she was dealing with.

"And how exactly am I odd?" a voice asked from the doorway.

Matilda closed her eyes, knowing this was the exact moment she would be sacked, and her good job would be gone. She would be back in the fields with her parents, toiling over land that may or may not produce a crop to the lord's satisfaction. "Excuse me?" If she played stupid, perhaps he would be lenient.

"You said the son left at home was odd. I am that son, and I would like to know just exactly how I am odd. I find myself very normal." Robert grinned at the new girl working for his parents. Aye, he was odd. Who else could make objects fly through the air at will?

"I am so sorry, milord. I did not see you there." Matilda waited for the ax to fall, wondering if it would be the proverbial ax or a real one. He was certainly in his rights to have her executed for saying something so rude.

"Apparently not." Robert shook his head.

"Mayhap you should be more careful when you are talking about people . . . make sure they are not standing close by." Robert stepped into the room, fascinated by how pretty the girl was. Her skin looked so soft and perfect. He wanted to touch her.

"I will in future, sir." Matilda was not sure if she should curtsy or just throw herself on the floor at his feet, begging for his mercy.

"You know you will need to be punished for your bad behavior, do not you?" he asked.

Matilda heard Mary giggle behind her and wondered what had happened to the girl. Why would she be laughing at such a thing? She had thought they were building a friendship. "Aye, sir."

Robert smiled at her. "Now what should that punishment be?" He stroked his chin as if contemplating a great mystery. "Mayhap you should have to eat your noon meal with me."

Matilda blinked at him. "Eat my meal with you?" How was that a punishment?

"Aye, you have to accompany me for lunch. I think that is a fitting punishment. If you are going to be talking about me, you have every right to learn more about me, so you can speak truth." Robert winked at Mary, who was still laughing. "I will come to find you just before the meal. Be ready to sit with the family." With those words, he was gone, stopping just out of view and sitting down.

"Robert?" his mother asked from behind him. "Is something wrong?"

Robert shook his head, laughing. "Not in the way you mean, Mother."

"Then what is it? Why are you not outside training with your men?"

"Would you believe I just met the woman I am going to marry?" he asked.

She grinned at him. "The new maid? She reads, you know." Her face told him how much she approved of his choice.

"I am not surprised. She is eating lunch with the family today as my guest." Robert got to his feet. "It is too bad Grandmother is not here. Her powers may be able to calm my rapidly beating heart."

His mother stood on tiptoe and kissed his cheek. "You do not have a need of being healed, son. Falling in love is one of the most natural things in the whole world." She patted his arm. "Now go and train. You should speak to your father."

He frowned for a moment. "Is not this the day we were to ride so you could let Aunt Christiana know all is well and get the news from home?" He had never met his aunt, but he had heard stories of her his entire life. His grandmother had visited for a month at least once a year, but his aunts had not. He knew his aunt Christiana, his grandmother's sister, had the power to speak to people in their minds. His aunt Eva, his grandmother's other sister, had the power to make illusions appear before people they believed were real.

She frowned at him. "It is the day we are supposed to ride. Let me take your father with me today instead. We will pack a picnic lunch."

He grinned. "Trying to leave me alone with the new maid, Mother?"

"Me? I have never been known as a matchmaker."

"Not to anyone but your children." He leaned down and hugged her. "Stay safe on your journey and thank you for the opportunity to be alone with her. I just wish I knew her name . . ."

"Matilda. Her name is Matilda, and she has my permission to borrow any book that interests her." His mother strode out of the castle then, and he knew she was off to tell his father she wanted him to ride with her to speak to her aunt.

Robert was left alone in the great hall of the castle, a smile upon his face.

Matilda looked over at Mary, her eyes

still wide. "Why did you not help me? You just stood there laughing!"

Mary grinned. "Because I know this family. When he said he would have to punish you, I could do nothing but laugh. I knew that was not what would happen. Robert is a good man."

"But . . . he said he is punishing me by making me eat the noon meal with him. What will he do?" Matilda had heard stories about lords who took advantage of their female staff.

"He will have a meal with you, and you will get to eat the meal meant for the family, not for the staff. I am sure it will be a lovely, enjoyable meal, and you will get to know the people who employ us. I wish I was invited!" Mary grinned at her, getting back to her work. "There is nothing to worry about. His parents will be right there."

"But . . . the stories about him . . ."

"Aye, he is odd. He treats servants as equals. I have never seen anything odder than that, have you?"

Matilda did not respond, her mind on the face of the man whom she had met a short while before. Her mother had warned her against falling for one of the members of the family she worked for, but how could she help it? He had a strong, handsome face, and he had shown her attention. She closed her eyes,

13

saying a prayer that she would be able to hold out until she went home on Sunday. Falling at the feel of her employer's youngest son would not be the way to keep her job.

Robert had a hard time paying attention to his training that morning. With his father gone, he was leading the different exercises, but his mind was not on training at all. Nay, it was on the pretty new maid. He wanted to ask her a million questions, and he did not want to have to wait until the noon meal to do it.

Never had he met a woman who looked so right to him. He knew his parents did not care if he married a noblewoman or a peasant. His own sister had been adopted from peasant parents long before he was born. She had always been treated as if she had been born a noblewoman.

When it was finally time for the meal, he called a halt to the training. "You may have a longer meal break than usual," he called out. "Twice as long would be perfect!" He did not stand around listening to his men cheer. Instead he went into the castle to find the pretty maid. Matilda. Even her name rolled off his tongue. She was going to be his, and he did not even care what she had to say about it.

He found her a moment later in a smaller sitting room, polishing the furniture. "It is time for your punishment, Matilda." Robert kept his voice stern, but he could not keep the smile from his face.

Matilda turned to him with a smile, trying to act like the meal she was to share with him did not frighten her at all. "I am ready, milord."

He offered her his arm, and she was startled at first, but she took it, walking with him to the great hall for their meal. "Tell me about yourself, Matilda. How long have you worked here?"

"Today is my first day. It is a beautiful place to work."

"And a beautiful place to live. Have you moved into the castle?" He arrived at the big table in the great hall and made sure he sat beside her.

"Where are you parents?" she asked, startled.

"They went to talk to my aunt. Have you moved into the castle?" He repeated his question, determined to learn everything he could about her.

"Aye, I took the room of Agnes, who married recently." Matilda was relatively certain he would have no idea anyone named Agnes had ever worked there, but she told him whose room she had anyway. Mayhap someone would know.

"Ah! I was at her wedding on Saturday. There was much dancing and merriment."

"You attended the wedding of a servant?" Her eyes were wide as she questioned him.

"Aye, I did. In our household, we treat servants as members of the family."

She studied him for a moment as Alice served them their meal. She had put their food all into one trencher, and she smiled at Matilda, letting her know that the other staff did not mind where she was eating. "That is very odd, milord."

"Aye, it is when you think about how most things are done, but my family tends to have secrets they do not want others to know about. By treating our servants as family, we have their loyalty, and they do not tell our family's secrets." He reached out and cut off a piece of the chicken in the trencher.

"And what are those secrets?" she asked. She could not stop herself if she wanted to. All her life she had heard whispers about the secrets of the family in the castle, but no one had known exactly what those secrets were!

"Are you ready for our secrets?" he asked her softly. "Are you ready to swear undying loyalty and keep the secret until your death, if that is required of you?"

She swallowed hard, almost afraid of what the big secret would entail. "Aye, milord. I am ready."

"My mother has the ability to control the weather. I have seen it rain, snow, and blow wind indoors more times than I can count."

She blinked at him for a moment before laughing. "it is not possible!"

He went on as if she had not interrupted. "And I have the ability to move things with my mind."

She shook her head, a huge smile on her face. "Oh, but you are funny."

"May I?" he asked.

Matilda grinned, waiting for him to do something. She knew it was impossible. If someone could do such a thing, why they would have to be a witch, and they would not be tolerated by the church. He and his family were in good standing with the church. "Aye, please."

Robert did not have to look at her to see her laughter. She did not believe him, and he understood that. Not many would. His family was odd. His father was the seventh son of a seventh son, going as far back as the family knew. Definitely back into their Viking history. When his father had married his mother—a woman descended from a long line of druids, his father's luck as the seventh son had combined with his mother's druid heritage . . . and he was born with the power to move objects with his mind. It was odd, and he was the first to admit it.

He looked straight ahead as he picked up a chair from the other side of the table, lifting it onto the end of the table and setting it down.

Matilda gasped. "How did you do that?"

"I just told you. I have the ability to move things with my mind. I know it sounds like a story for children, but it is not. it is true in my case."

CHAPTER TWO

Matilda sat staring at him, wondering if Robert was playing an elaborate prank on her. Were there thin ropes attached to the chair? There had to be. There was no other explanation for what she had just seen. "How did you do that? Really?"

He sighed. "Just like I told you." He concentrated on a small piece of meat in their trencher, commanding it to flow through the air and to her mouth. "Open up, my sweet."

She did as she was told, but she did not know why. As she chewed the food, she stared at him in awe. "How long have you been able to do that?" she asked, still astonished at what she was seeing. No wonder people called him odd!

"There is a story my mother likes to tell. At the time, they had no idea I would develop a power. You see, in my mother's family, most females are born with power, but not all. Never has a male been born with powers. In my father's family, the seventh son gets extra luck. I know that sounds strange, but the seventh son will always know which way to dodge in a sword fight or which path to take to find a treasure. So when my father married my mother, the powers seemed to combine, and I have this strange ability to move things with my mind."

"But . . ."

He laughed. "I know it is strange. I think so as well. Anyway, when I was four months old, my mother had just fed me, and I was lying on her bed. I kicked my feet and a blanket flew from across the room to cover me up. So she removed the blanket, and I did it again. And again. She called my father, and he watched me move the blanket, and they both just stared at me in surprise. They were not expecting to have any children with true powers."

"But they did. What about your brothers?"

He shook his head. "Nay, none of them have powers. Just me."

"You do not fear that I will tell someone?"

"Of course I do. But you are a member of my family now."

"Where do the powers come from?" She resisted the urge to cross herself for the second time that day. His powers were wonderful . . . yet frightening all at once.

Robert grinned. "Go ahead and cross yourself. It will not offend me. I have no idea where the powers come from, but my family has always assumed they come from God. My mother wears a cross, as does her mother." He picked up a chain from inside his chain mail and held it out to her. "As do I." He squeezed the cross in his hand, showing her that it had not burned his palm. "See?"

"It is very strange, milord."

"Aye, it is. But I have no complaints about it. It is a power that anyone would be pleased to have. It helps mightily in a battle."

Matilda pictured him sword fighting with someone and their sword soaring out of their hands to stab another enemy, and she bit her lip against the laughter bubbling up inside her. "I can just picture it, milord."

His eyes met hers, sharing the laughter with her. "I see that you understand my meaning."

She nodded. "I do. It would be something to watch."

"I am glad you agreed to have the noon meal with me today."

"Agreed?" She gave him a surprised look. "I did not agree. It was my punishment, if you will recall."

He grinned. "I am sure Mary told you that It was not a true punishment. That you would just be eating with me."

Matilda frowned. "She said I would be eating with your parents as well. Where are your parents, milord?"

"They went off to talk to my aunt. Mother decided a picnic would be nice when she realized I wanted to eat my meal alone with you."

"Alone? You wanted to eat alone?"

Robert nodded. "I plan to get to know you better, Matilda."

She shook her head. "My mother told me not to allow any member of the family get too close to me."

"I am not planning to take advantage of you. I want you to trust me enough to agree to be my wife." He understood her mother's concerns, but he had no improper intentions. He wanted to spend the rest of his life with her.

She immediately started choking on the food in her mouth, and he handed her a tankard of water. "Wife?"

He nodded. "I heard you talking about me and decided to tease you a little, but when I saw your face, I knew."

"Knew?"

"That you were meant to be mine." He said the words so simply that she stared at him in shock.

"Do you say things like that to all the new maids, milord?"

"Actually, I have never told anyone that I meant to marry her. You are definitely the first." Robert watched her face, hoping she had believe him. The words were true, and he very much wanted her to agree right there and then to planning a wedding.

She shook her head. "I do not think you know what you are saying. I am the daughter of a serf. You are the son of a nobleman. We cannot marry." But she would not be his mistress. She had more pride than that. If she had to, she would return to the hovel where she had grown up and move back in with her parents.

"You do not know my family. My mother met my father when he took her a sick peasant child to heal. They healed her and ended up raising her. She is my only sister. That is how my family is. We do not care about class."

"But adopting a peasant is very different than marrying one. I am sure your parents would not approve." She shook her head. "I do not even know you."

"Well, we will spend time getting to know each

other. I need you to know that I feel strongly about you becoming my bride." He picked up a piece of meat and held it to her lips, waiting for her to take it from his hand. She held up her hand to take it, and he shook his head. "Not like that."

Blushing, she took the meat from his fingers with her mouth, careful not to touch his fingers with her lips. "Why?"

"Because you are beautiful. Because that is the way it needs to be. I have no other reasons." He got to his feet. "Thank you for the pleasant noon meal. I expect you here for supper so my parents can get to know you. I will fetch you when it is time."

"But I am supposed to eat with the other servants!"

Robert grinned. "That is how it normally works, but not tonight." He walked away, whistling a happy tune under his breath. He knew he was an odd man when you considered that he was a member of the nobility, but he simply did not care. She would be his bride. His children would not be any less noble for it.

As Matilda watched Robert walk away, she was flummoxed. How on earth was she supposed to hold her ground when a man like that was trying to convince her that she was meant to be his bride? What would her mother say?

She hurried back to her duties, finding Mary on

her hands and knees in one of the many sitting rooms, and she joined her.

"What did he say to you?" Mary asked.

"He told me I am meant to be his bride." Matilda still could not believe it, and as she spoke the words aloud, she knew she would not believe her if she heard it.

Mary laughed long and hard. "I had a feeling it would be something of that sort. The Lains are special people!"

"I do not know what to do. My mother told me that if any of the men in the family showed a special interest in me, I was to run straight home." Matilda wondered if she should already be on her way.

"She meant if one was trying to force his attentions on you. It sounds like Robert wants to legitimately court you, and that cannot be a bad thing. Your mother would want your life to be better by marrying a nobleman."

Matilda shook her head. "I am not so sure. She does not trust noblemen at all."

"Well, of course not. Very few serfs do. But that does not make them not want to be just like them." Mary sighed. "If Robert wanted to marry me, I would happily agree. He is handsome, intelligent, and a good man. I think you should give him a chance."

"I will think about it."

Matilda hurried to her room to straighten her appearance just before supper time, and then she went down to the kitchen to see if she could be of assistance. Alice shooed her away. "Lord Robert has taken special notice of you, Matilda. You need to be available to him."

"What if I do not want his special attentions?" Matilda asked, still unsure of how she felt about the entire situation.

Alice just laughed. "Of course you want them, girl. You are not a halfwit!"

Matilda frowned. "No, I am not a halfwit."

Alice pushed a platter toward her. "Carry this out to the table, and then stay there so Lord Robert can find you."

Matilda did as she was told, putting the large platter on the table and looking around the great hall. His mother came toward her with a smile on her face. "Robert tells me he is revealed some family secrets to you."

"Aye, milady. He says you can make it snow or rain inside." Matilda wondered if it was possible or if Robert had simply said some things to shock her. She had to believe it was possible if he could move objects with his mind.

The older woman smiled, and a gentle snow fell in the great hall. "I really can."

"Oh my!" Matilda shook her head. "I should not have doubted him."

"Robert also tells me that he wants to get to know you better, and that is why you are having supper with us. Well, he said he is going to marry you, but we will have to see how that works out."

"You would not hate the idea?" Matilda thought that as soon as he mentioned the idea to his parents, it would be argued with.

"Not at all. We are just happy Robert has found someone he wants to spend the rest of his life with. I hope that you feel the same after spending some time with him and getting to know him. And I want you to know that as the woman he is courting, you have the right to stay in one of our guest rooms and not work any longer. The choice is truly yours."

"I will continue to work." Matilda shook her head. "I would not know what to do with my time if I did not."

Lady Lina laughed. "I assure you, there is always enough to do. Mayhap I will steal you from Alice and allow you to follow me around so I can teach you how to run this household when I move away into the home I will live in once Robert marries."

"Why would not you stay here? This is where you have raised your family!"

"Aye, it is, but it is also where I know my son will raise his family. There is no need for me to stay here when there is a perfectly good house still on Lain land."

Matilda had never met a family quite like his. They were willing to give up the home where they had lived for many years so their youngest son could raise his children there. Why not just share it as most families did? "I will not argue with you about your family's traditions."

Lady Lina laughed. "I argued with my mother-in-law about them. Why would you not argue with me?"

"You did?"

"Of course. It seemed silly that she would give up the house where she had raised her children so I could move in and have seven sons. I am glad she did, though. It is a good tradition, though I did not realize it until I was already expecting my third son."

"Seven sons is a lot of children. Were you never worried?"

"About giving birth?" Lady Lina shook her head. "My mother is a healer. I am a healer with potions and herbs, but my mother heals with her touch. She came and stayed with me through each of my pregnancies. I was always very ill from them."

Matilda frowned. "My mother has had seven children die. I am the only one to live to adulthood."

"It is sad, but so many families have experienced the same. Without my mother's healing powers, I doubt if I would have lived to give birth to my first son, let alone seven. She was here a great deal because I had seven children in ten years." Lady Lina smiled. "So when one of my sons went tumbling down the stairs, she was there to heal him before he awoke. She was there when another son fell off a horse. Mother made things easier."

"It sounds like it." Matilda looked over Lady Lina's shoulder as Robert walked toward them. Now that she had spoken to his mother and determined that his interest in her was real, she was shy in his presence.

He walked toward her and took her hand, kissing the back of it. "Good evening, Matilda."

"Milord."

"Please call me Robert." He smiled down at her, his blue-gray eyes dancing. "It would make me very happy."

"I could not! It would not be right."

His mother smiled. "Call him Robert. Trust me, it is fine."

Matilda could not believe his mother was so calm about her using his first name. "But he is my better."

Lady Lina shook her head. "No, he is not. We are all equal despite the circumstances of our birth. I happen to know you are an intelligent young woman, and I would be pleased to have you marry my son."

Her husband came and stood beside Lady Lina, his arm around her. "Are we giving the 'all people are born equal' lecture again? I just do not see the idea catching on, wife, as much as *we* believe it to be the truth." He smiled at Matilda. "I am Lord Alex, Robert's father."

Matilda was not sure what the proper thing to do was, so she bowed her head. "Milord."

Alex looked at Robert and nodded. "You are right son. She is a beauty."

Robert grinned. "And she does not think she can use my given name. Please tell her to call me Robert."

Alex smiled. "Call him Robert. Standing on ceremony when he plans to marry you is silly."

Matilda looked at Robert, surprised he had talked to his parents about marrying her when he had just met her that day. "Do you tell your parents every thought that flits through your head?"

Robert laughed, joined by both of his parents. "Not always, but I thought they might want some warning that I planned to marry soon. it will give them time to pack their belongings and get ready to move."

"Mayhap you should talk to my parents about this. I am not sure they will be as enthusiastic as yours." She was sure they would not, but she was not about to tell him that right then.

"Mayhap not. But that does not mean my mind will be changed." He wanted her parents to be happy that he was falling in love with their daughter, but if they were not, it would not stop him from marrying her. Only she could do that.

"Shall we eat?" his mother asked.

Robert pulled a chair out for Matilda, and she sat down uncomfortably. It was strange having a member of the nobility use his manners to court her. "Thank you," she said, trying to be polite, but not sure if she should say something.

While they ate, Robert and his parents peppered her with questions.

"Where did you learn to read?" his mother asked.

Matilda bit her lip, unsure if she should answer truthfully. "I am not sure I should say."

"We believe women should read," his father told her. "Our daughter has been reading since she was three years old."

"Really?" Matilda asked, surprised. "I was taught

by our parish priest. He said that he did not think reading should only be for men, and he asked me if I wanted to learn. I was very excited and so were my parents. They thought it would be a way for me to better myself if it were possible at all."

"So your parents like the idea of you bettering yourself?" Robert asked, a gleam in his eye. "Then they will certainly like the idea of you marrying me."

"I am not as certain as you are," she said, shaking her head. "I suppose the only way to know is to talk to them. They expect me home every Sunday."

"I hope to be married to you by Sunday!" he said. "We should go talk to them tomorrow."

"We cannot marry so quickly! Why would we do such a thing?" From what she knew, you spent months and months planning a wedding once you decided to marry. Why would they marry in just a few days?

"Some people wait a long time, and some people do not. We married within two days of meeting each other," his mother said. "My father was not thrilled, but he certainly is now. He and Alex have become fast friends over the years."

Lord Alex nodded. "It is true. Her father hated me at first. It took the two of us worrying over Lina and her illness through pregnancies for us to become close."

"I see." Matilda looked down for a moment. "Were you raised as a serf as well, milady?"

Lady Lina shook her head. "Nay, I was raised by a Norman father and a Saxon mother in a castle bigger than this one."

"Do you ever go home and visit your family?" Matilda asked, wondering if she would be asked to give up her family entirely if she was to marry into this family.

"No, but only because it is a three-day ride from here. My parents have come to visit us often. It was hard to travel with seven sons and a daughter." Lady Lina smiled. "As soon as Robert marries and takes over the running of the castle and army here, I am sure we will be able to visit."

Matilda could not imagine a family that large. "Did you always want to have so many children?"

Lady Lina shrugged. "I knew when I married Alex that there would be seven sons and no daughters. it is the fate of each of the seventh sons of the family. We adopted our daughter so that I could have one. Well, we would have adopted her anyway, but I like to joke it was my way to get around the seven sons and no daughters."

Matilda looked at Robert, blinking rapidly. "So to marry you means seven sons and no daughters? There is never any other way the family grows?"

"My brothers may have all daughters or all sons or a combination of both, but we know I will have seven sons. No more and no less. And all seven sons will live to adulthood." Robert shrugged. "it is the way it is been for many generations."

"Oh my. I have never heard of a family that was so set in how things would go. I am not sure I am ready to commit to having no daughters."

His mother smiled at her. "You can always find an orphan and keep her like we did."

Matilda sighed. As handsome as Robert was and as kind and loving as his family seemed, it did not feel like the right decision for her to make. "I see."

Robert watched her, realizing that she was not ready to commit to everything, and he could certainly understand why. She barely knew him and did not have the luck that his family had. He knew as soon as he saw her she needed to be his. He would just have to work on convincing her, and if that meant convincing her with kisses and with long romantic walks, he would make it happen.

His father's eyes met his, and he knew his father was thinking the same thing he was. His parents liked her. That much was readily obvious. Now he just had to convince her that they were meant to be, and then convince her father that he should be allowed to court her. How hard could it be?

He looked over at her and saw that she was looking completely bewildered as she looked from him to his mother to his father and back to him again. It might be harder than he was anticipating, but what did it matter if it was difficult? All the things in life that were worth having were hard.

CHAPTER THREE

As soon as they were finished eating, Robert turned to Matilda. "I would like to walk with you, if you will favor me with a bit more of your time."

Matilda frowned at him, trying to decide what he really wanted from her. Why was he using his best manners to invite a maid to go on a walk with him? He could have just ordered her to, and she would have done it. Why make it seem like she had a choice in the matter?

Finally, she nodded. "Aye, I will walk with you." He held his hand out for hers, and after hesitating a moment, she put her hand in his. She felt a rush of emotions flood through her body at his touch, but she did what she could to hide it. This man had a power over her that she had never expected. "Thank you for allowing me to share your meal, Lord Alex and Lady Lina."

Lina grinned at her. "I certainly hope it will become something you do often."

Matilda nodded her head once in recognition of the statement before she was pulled from the room and out of the castle by Robert. "You are being rude to your parents, milord!"

"Robert. You must use my name or pay the forfeit."

She almost laughed. The man thought eating with him was a suiting punishment. What would he consider a forfeit? "Lord Robert, I do not think it is fitting for me to use your given name . . . "

Robert waited until they were outside walls surrounding the castle before turning on her. "*Lord* Robert? Did you say *Lord* Robert?"

Matilda could not help but giggle in response. There was something about this man that made her want to forget all her duties and just follow him around. She knew her parents would not be pleased. "You must have misheard me, milord. I would never call you something you had not asked me to call you."

Robert wrapped one arm around her waist. "Do not lie to me, wench!"

She giggled again, her hands coming up to rest on his shoulders. "I beg your pardon, *milord*. It shall not happen again!" She could not help but emphasize the word, milord.

He growled and leaned toward her face. "Now you must pay the forfeit!"

"A lock of my hair? A piece of my toenail? Perhaps a feather from my pillow!" She could not believe she was giving him ideas for the forfeit he asked for, but the game was such fun. Never had she simply enjoyed herself this way. Life was about work for most people she knew, and he was showing her a whole new side of things.

He leaned down further until his lips were hovering just above hers. "A kiss."

She could feel his breath against her lips. Never had she kissed a man. Her parents had kept her sheltered as much as they could. One of them had always been with her until that very day. "But . . . I know nothing of kisses." She had never even wanted to kiss a man, and all of a sudden, she could not take her eyes from his lips. The idea of having them brush against hers made her heart beat faster.

"Oh? Then you should not have disobeyed me!"

She frowned up at him, wondering if he would be satisfied with the kind of kiss she would give her mother. She knew of no other kind, so she pulled his head down and pressed a kiss to his cheek, feeling very bold. "There, I have paid my forfeit."

Robert could not help but grin. "That was *not* a kiss, Matilda. That was merely a brush of your lips across my cheek."

"It is the only kind of kiss I know, mi—" She stopped herself before the full word was out, but he caught it. It felt good to tease him as she was. This man . . . he was something special.

"You are trying to raise my ire!"

She shook her head. "No, I would not. I just . . . I have never kissed a man. Only my parents, and they do not count."

"Then you will learn to kiss this very night." He took her hand and resumed their walk, leaving her surprised.

"I will?" Why was he walking again if he intended to kiss her? Was not the spot where they stood a good one for learning how to kiss?

"You will."

"What if I choose not to kiss you? Would that anger you?" She had to wonder what he would be like if angered.

Robert sighed. "I will never force anything upon you, but it would sadden me a great deal. If I am sad, then my mother becomes sad. You do not want it raining inside the castle, do you?"

ROBERT

She laughed. "Does it rain inside the castle when your mother is sad?"

"If she is not paying attention it does. When she met my father, she immediately made it snow inside in the middle of the summer." He grinned at her.

"What emotion is she feeling when it snows?"

"Embarrassment. And then of course she was more embarrassed because she would made it snow!"

Matilda laughed. "I think the powers in your family are fascinating, but I would not want them. I would probably do horrible things without meaning to!" She could not imagine knowing how to use a power like that. It sounded wonderful and frightening all at once. No, she would leave the powers for others.

Robert looked down at her, walking beside him in the moonlight. He had never met a woman he was so drawn to! "If you had all the time in the world and no responsibilities, what would you do?" he asked.

"I would read every book I could find," she answered without hesitation. "I might even write a book myself. Has a woman ever written a book?"

"I do not know. I have never met a woman who was quite so passionate about reading. Will you teach our sons to read?" he asked, watching her carefully to see how she responded to his mention of

41

them having children, as if it was a foregone conclusion.

She made a face at him. "I have not agreed to have your sons, if you will remember."

"I could order you to marry me." He would not, but he wanted to know what her reaction would be to his threat.

"And know that you were trapping a woman who may not want to be your bride? I do not think you would. I think you would rather find a way to *convince* me to agree to be your bride." Matilda did not know him well yet, but she already knew that much. He was too gentle to be willing to force a woman into marriage with him.

"No, I would not do that. You are right. But I do want to go and meet your parents on the morrow. Mother said that you could leave the castle without a problem tomorrow. Will you do it? Introduce me to your parents?"

Matilda bit her lips. "My mother was very worried the son of the lord of the castle would show too much of an interest in me. It frightened her a great deal. I do not know how she would feel if we went to her and told her you want to marry me." Something inside her made her want to find out. Could she be starting to fall under his spell?

"I would think she would be relieved that my

intentions were good and not malicious." Robert spotted the bench he would been walking toward and sat down on it, pulling her down beside him. "I would like to try."

She sighed. "I will take you to my parents, but I do not want you to think they will be happy that you want to marry me."

"We shall see." He turned to her on the bench, cupping her face in his huge hands. "Now, let us see to that kissing lesson."

She looked up at him, not sure what to say to that. She had always been known for being quick with a comeback when someone said something to her. It was considered most unladylike, but she had never pretended to be a lady. His eyes seemed very large as she stared into them, and she was a touch frightened. Mostly she knew he would never hurt her.

He lowered his head slowly, and she felt as if her heart would stop beating if his mouth never touched hers. When they finally did connect, she gasped softly against his lips, and he traced her lips with his tongue.

Matilda had not known that much feeling was inside her, and she was certain it was not until he touched her. He made her feel things that would have been impossible before, but now they would not stop shooting through her body. Finally, she dragged her mouth away, her chest heaving. "Must needs catch my breath!"

His hand stayed on her shoulder, toying with her hair, as he fought for control of his own body. The wedding needed to be soon. He would not be able to hold out long. The passion was just too much.

"You will break your fast with my family in the morning, and then the two of us will head to your parents' home. I must speak with them about the feelings I have for you and about my intention to marry you."

She stared at him for another moment, but she knew she had no willpower at all where he was concerned. She needed to agree, so they could marry quickly. It was in that moment that she realized she had no choice. If he did not command her to marry him, her body would do it for him. "I will take you to them."

"And you will marry me?" he asked for the first time. He had been hinting about it all day, but it was the first time he actually asked her.

"I do not know. I must talk to my parents about it. They may choose to keep me there rather than send me back here to marry you."

He did not think such a thing was likely, but he did not argue with her. She knew her parents better than he did, and she knew how they felt about the nobility. He could only guess based on the peasants he had known in the past. "May I walk you to your chamber?"

She shook her head. "No, you may not. It would be terribly forward of you to do so. Instead, you may walk me to the entrance to the servants' quarters and say goodnight there."

"You are getting very bossy, Matilda." Robert loved that she was asserting her opinion and no longer running from him in fear. She seemed to have come to an understanding that he would not hurt her. He was thrilled. Now he just had to convince her parents. How hard could it be?

They held hands as they walked back to the castle and in through the servants' entrance. She walked to the door that led up to the chamber she was using. "Goodnight. It has been a lovely day." She said the words because she knew they were expected of her, but she realized they were true. It had been a very lovely day, and she had enjoyed every minute of it. Even dusting and cleaning his home was so much easier than the field work she had done with her parents.

Robert pulled her to him. "You still have not used my Christian name. It is Robert. Practice it all night because I expect to hear it from your lips in the morning."

She laughed softly, seeing him better inside because candles were still lit around the kitchen. "I will do my best."

He leaned down and brushed his lips against hers firmly. "Dream of me, Matilda, for I shall be dreaming of you." He watched as she hurried through the door, all but running from him. He knew her well enough now that he knew she was running from her own feelings more than she was running from him.

It was wonderful to know she was afraid of her feelings because he knew he was afraid of his.

In her room, Matilda sank into the bed, finding it more comfortable than any place she had ever slept. This job, this castle, this man. All were changing her life. Mayhap a little too fast.

Matilda woke early the following morning, as was her habit. She stretched and laid in bed for a moment, trying to remember where she was. And then it all came rushing back, and Robert's face appeared in her mind. She thought about him for a moment as she got up and readied herself for her day of work.

Surely, he would have forgotten all about wanting to marry her by today. He must have lost his mind when he decided she was the only woman for him.

She would go downstairs and act as if nothing had happened with him the day before, and she would do her job. It was the only thing she could do. Hopefully the others would not be too sorry for her when he forgot who she was.

When Matilda got down to the kitchen, she immediately reported to Alice. "How may I help?"

Alice's eyes grew wide as she looked at her. "Lady Lina has already been here to talk to me this morning. Lord Robert is insisting that you move to one of the empty chambers meant for family on the other side of the castle." She locked eyes on someone behind Matilda. "Mary, help Matilda move her things please."

"My possessions are few, and I need no help moving them. Truly, though, I think I should stay where I am. At least for a while." Matilda was not sure why everyone was in such a hurry to get her out of the servants' quarters.

Alice shook her head. "You may defy him all you like in private, but I will follow my orders. Mary?"

Mary hurried forward. "A room was prepared for

you yestereve while you were dining with the family." She turned around and hurried up the stairs, leaving Matilda with no choice but to follow her.

"I did not know another room had been made ready. Did you do it?"

Mary nodded. "Aye, and I was thrilled to do it for my friend. I cannot believe your station in life is changing so quickly. Lady Lina said you were no longer to be considered help. You will be following her around and learning to run the castle instead."

"I will?" Matilda shook her head. Lady Lina had suggested it the night before, but Matilda had thought she was joking.

"Aye, you did not know?" Mary's eyes were filled with mirth. She quickly took the few possessions Matilda had brought with her and bundled them together. "You are going to need new dresses as well. Mayhap you will ask Lady Lina if I can be the one to help you with them. I think we will work well together."

"Oh, aye! If I must have a maid, I would prefer it be one I can call my friend."

Mary nodded. "I was hoping you would say that." She hurried out of the room, Matilda following her. "There is no connection between the two parts of the castle. You can only reach the servants' quarters from the kitchen, but you can only reach the upstairs where the family lives from the great hall."

Matilda simply followed, learning all she could. When Mary started up the stairs on the other side, Matilda put her hand on her arm. "I do not feel like I should allow my things to be moved."

"You have no choice, Matilda. We do as we are told. Come on!" Mary continued her journey up the stairs and stopped at the second door at the top. "That is his parents' chamber," she said, nodding to the first door. "Yours will be right beside it. Lord Robert's is way down at the other end of the hall."

"Do his parents not trust him?" Matilda asked with a grin.

"Apparently his mother does not trust him where you are concerned." Mary pushed open the door and walked to the trunk at the foot of the bed, putting Matilda's meager belongings into it. "Now sit down and allow me to fix your hair for you. I know it is not something you are used to, but I can make it look much more beautiful, and then you can tell Lady Lina that I make a wonderful lady's maid."

Matilda felt like she was living in a dream. No one had ever fixed her hair but her mother or herself. She did as she was told and sat down, feeling Mary pluck the pins that held her hair up. "I will brush it first. Your hair is beautiful, Matilda."

Thirty minutes later, Matilda was headed down the stairs to break the fast with the family of the castle. Her hair was in an intricate knot at the back of her head, and she felt odd. This was not her life. She was an interloper. At least she was still wearing a dress she would brought with her; though she knew it made her stand out as a peasant, she was comfortable in it.

Lord Robert was waiting for her at the bottom of the stairs, and he offered his arm. She immediately tucked her hand into the curve of his arm and allowed him to escort her to the table. When they reached the table, she saw that his parents were already seated there. They had just been waiting for her. She was mortified that she would made them wait while Mary had played with her hair.

"Good morning. I beg your pardon for making you wait." Matilda wondered if they had send her right back to work where she belonged.

"Nonsense. It is my fault you were late. I made you move all your things this morning when you were not expecting it. I hope you will find your new chamber comfortable." Lady Lina smiled at her, making it clear she was not upset at all.

"Aye, of course I will, milady. It is the most beautiful room I have ever seen." Matilda did not even have to exaggerate. Yesterday the most beautiful room she had ever seen was the one she had slept in last night. Today, her standards were changing quickly.

"I am glad you like it. I want to have some more dresses made for you as well. Are you a good hand with a needle?"

Matilda nodded. "I am, but if I may ask, I would love for Mary to help me. She did my hair this morning."

Lady Lina nodded. "Sounds wonderful. She will be a good maid for you, I think."

Robert was sitting across from Matilda, and she looked over at him, trying to determine if he thought everything was moving too quickly. Matilda was more than a little overwhelmed by how fast her life was changing. "Does all this make you happy?"

He nodded. "But I would be much happier if you would use my given name. My mother is going to start thinking you do not approve of the name she gave me."

Matilda sighed. "It does not feel right calling you by your name. Robert." She forced the name out of her mouth and realized that it did feel right on her lips. Robert.

"That is the way! We are leaving right after we break the fast to go see your parents. We will take the carriage. I do not suppose you know how to ride?" he asked. it would make things simpler for him, because he preferred riding, but it was unlikely she had the skill.

She shook her head. "My family has never had enough wealth to own a horse."

Lady Lina shook her head. "You will learn to ride as soon as possible. It is one of the most freeing things that you can do. Galloping across a meadow with no saddle . . ."

Robert shook his head. "Matilda will use a saddle."

"I never have, and I am a very good rider." Lady Lina was smiling, making Matilda think this was an argument they had often.

"You have been riding your entire life, Mother. Matilda has never been atop a horse. She will need lessons from someone who will teach her to use a saddle and not ride bareback."

Lord Alex smiled at Matilda. "You will find my wife a better teacher, but she will most certainly try to teach you to ride with no saddle, which is the most *unladylike* way to ride."

Matilda looked between the two and shook her head. "I am not sure I am ready to learn to ride. A carriage is likely the best way for me to get around for a while."

Alex laughed. "She made her own decision and refused to do what the two of you want! Now what?"

Robert shrugged. "I do not really care if she never learns to ride a horse as long as she is willing to marry me."

"Let us see what my parents say first." She was certain her parents were going to insist she stay home and not go back to the castle. There had been too many rumors about the family for her parents to trust them with her.

"All right. We will go, and we will talk to your parents, but do not be surprised when they meet me and realize they love me and want to keep me as their own son." Robert grinned at her, lifting his glass in a toast.

Matilda looked over at Lady Lina. "Has he always displayed so much humility?"

"Oh aye. From the day of his birth, he has been just this humble."

"I was afraid of that." Matilda shook her head at Robert, wondering how her parents were going to respond to him.

CHAPTER FOUR

As soon as they had finished breaking the fast, Robert led Matilda out to the carriage he had waiting. He helped her up and then moved around to sit beside her, taking the leads. With a flick of his wrist, they were off. "You will have to guide me," he said to her, thrilled that she was sitting close enough that her arm was pressed against his. "I have never been there."

She nodded. "Follow the road to the right." She grew more and more nervous as they drove. "I am afraid my parents will be upset that we are coming to see them." Truly she had no idea how her parents would react. They had never expected any more than being a serf for their only living child.

"Well, I will do my best to make them understand that I want nothing but what is best for you." He glanced over at her. "Are you an only child?"

"In some ways. My mother had seven other children who all died before they reached adulthood. Some as babes. Some as small children. I am the only one to be old enough for her to worry about marrying."

"Do you remember any of them?"

She shook her head. "No, I was the youngest of them all. None were alive while I was. My mother is old. She had me when she was over thirty summers old!"

"That is not old," he responded. "My mother had me at twenty-nine summers, but I am older than you are."

"How old?" she asked. She knew not everyone liked to be asked questions about their age, but if he was considering courting and marrying her, then she had every right to know.

"Twenty-five summers." Robert looked over at Matilda. "Do you think that is too old?"

She shook her head. "Probably not." She pointed. "There! That is my home."

"Your parents' home," he responded. "Your new home is in the castle with me."

She smiled at him, doing her best not to contradict the man. "They are probably both in the field."

"We will walk out to them then."

Her eyes widened. "Mayhap you should wait inside while I go and fetch them." She could not imagine him walking across the field toward her parents. She could get them for him quite easily.

Robert shook his head. "Nay. I will walk with you. It is not like I am a weakling and cannot walk across a field."

"Well, you are getting old, milord."

He shook his head, getting down and walking around the carriage. Offering his hand to help her down, he said, "You might want to refrain from teasing me while we are trying to convince your parents we should marry. I am not sure how they will react." He secretly loved the way she teased, but only when they were alone and it was appropriate.

"I am not either." Yesterday, she was convinced they would hate the idea, and she did not have a problem with that. Now that he would kissed her, she could think of nothing but being his bride. She hoped they could convince her parents that it was the best thing for her, but she knew her mother had warned her just yesterday about getting involved with the son of the lord of the castle. That son was beside her and wanted to be her husband. How was she going to explain that?

This time it was she who led the way to their

destination, walking around the little house where she had always lived and toward the large fields her parents were the caretakers of. When she reached the field, she lifted her hand in a wave, and she immediately saw her mother drop her bucket of water and run toward her, her arms outstretched.

As Matilda embraced her mother, her mind raced to find the right way to explain why she was home. "Mother, I brought Robert Lain to meet you. He is the youngest son of Lord Alexander."

Her mother immediately bobbed a curtsey, looking nervous. "Milord."

"Please call me Robert."

Her mother shook her head. "Oh, I could not!"

Robert sighed. At least he now knew where Matilda got her stubbornness from. "I have come to speak with you and your husband. Is he close?"

Her mother looked from Matilda to Robert and then nodded. "Aye, I will go and get him."

"Let me do it, Mother. I do not want you to have to walk all that way when I can do it."

Her mother seemed to hesitate, and then she nodded. "All right. Go."

As Matilda ran off across the field, Robert smiled at her mother. "I want to marry her." He looked back at Matilda running so freely over the field. She was beautiful, and he never wanted to take his eyes off her.

She put her hand over her chest as if there was something wrong with her heart for just a moment. "Marry?"

He nodded. "I know it is sudden, but the people in my family tend to meet the person they are meant to spend their lives with, and they marry immediately. My parents knew one another for two days before they married." He knew it was a strange concept for most people to understand, but it was the only way he had ever known.

"I warned her about you . . ."

"I know you did. I appreciate you trying to protect her, but my parents are ready to accept her as their newest daughter, and I want her for my wife. I will inherit the castle as soon as I marry, so there is no worry about the home I will be able to provide for her." He hoped getting her mother on his side before her father returned would help him be able to convince her father. He could see Matilda walking back toward him with a man who was slightly stooped over. "May I have your support?"

She stared at him. "Why would you want to marry her? You do not need to marry to bed a serf."

"No, I do not, but I do not just want to bed her. I want to spend the rest of my life with her, and I want her to bear my children." Robert had to convince her it was the truth. He knew Matilda desperately wanted her parents to support any future marriage.

She slowly nodded. "I will support you."

He smiled. "Thank you." He felt as if he had climbed a mountain when he got Matilda's mother's agreement. He was halfway there.

When Matilda returned with the old man, Robert turned his attention to her father. "I am Robert, youngest son of Lord Alexander. I will inherit his castle as soon as I marry, and I would like to marry your daughter."

Matilda's eyes grew wide as Robert got straight to the point. She had not yet taken the time to explain why they were there.

Her father looked at Matilda. "Do you wish to marry this man?"

Matilda bit her lip before nodding. "Aye, I do."

"Then marry him. I have no objection to you marrying a man who will take good care of you. You have my blessing." With those words, her father turned to go back to his field. He was obviously finished with the conversation.

"I would like to marry her two days hence. Would you both come to the castle for the wedding feast?"

Her parents exchanged a glance. "We would not want to shame her. We have no clothes that are worthy of a feast. She may marry you, but I think we should stay away," her mother said softly.

"I would like for you to be there," Matilda said. "Please."

Her mother shook her head. "No, child. It is not for us. You enjoy yourself and come to visit us when you can."

Matilda felt her tears falling. She felt as if this was her parents' way to say goodbye to her. She was not wanting to end her relationship with them. "I will come often."

Her mother smiled and nodded, hugging her close. "I love you. Be happy, my child." She turned away and walked back to the field where she would work.

Matilda looked at Robert. "They are acting as if they will never see me again."

Robert was quiet for a moment as he realized what her parents were doing. They were giving her the opportunity to leave them in her past. She would seem to all to be a high-born lady if they were not around. She was educated, and she would be wearing the finest clothes as soon as they married. He put his arm around her and led her back to the carriage, knowing he would have to find a way for her parents to continue to be part of her life.

She was quiet on the ride back to the castle.

When they reached their destination, Robert jumped down and helped Matilda to the ground. "Go find Mary. You two will need to start sewing immediately. I will talk to Mother and have her start getting everything ready for a wedding feast."

"I would like a portion of the feast to be taken to my parents," she said softly.

"I was already planning to do that very thing." He looked at her, hating the sadness that was etched on her face. He pulled her to him and held her close. "We will do all we can for them to continue to be part of your life."

She looked up at him with surprise. "Why?"

"Because I can see that it will make you happy. Your happiness means everything to me, Matilda. I will see to it." He turned and led the horses to the stable, handing them off to a stable boy before going in to talk to his mother. He assumed Matilda was off doing what he would instructed.

———

Matilda found Mary and hurried up the stairs with her. She took her to her room and explained how her parents had acted.

Mary nodded. "Aye, my parents were the same way when I came to work here. This is a higher station than they were in, so they knew I would never go back."

"Have you?"

Mary shook her head. "No, the people I work with here have become my family. I have not returned."

"I do not want it to be like that for my parents, but Robert wants to marry in two days, so I have to start making dresses. I have been given permission for you to be my personal maid, and we are to start making new clothes for me immediately."

Mary clapped her hands together. "This will help me a lot. You will be the lady of the house, and I will be your maid. I will be moving up several ranks overnight."

"The others will not be upset, will they?"

"Alice told me to talk to you. She said that we got on well enough that it could be what I needed to better myself."

Matilda smiled. "I am glad it is working out well for you. We must go find Lady Lina so we can get started sewing."

"Matilda?" Mary asked.

Matilda stopped and turned back to her friend. "Aye?"

"Will you be happy with Lord Robert?"

Matilda bit her lip, thinking about the question.

"I believe I will. I feel more for him than I have ever felt for a man. I cannot say that I love him because I barely know him, but I do believe love will come in time."

"Then let us go get you some fabric so we can make you dresses." Mary smiled and led the way out of the room and down the stairs to Lady Lina. As soon as she saw Robert's mother, she called out to her. "Lady Lina!"

Lina turned and smiled at the two girls walking toward her. "Aye, how can I help you?"

"If there is to be a wedding two days hence, we are going to need to start sewing immediately. Do you have any fabric we may use?" Mary asked.

"Of course. I keep a trunk with fabrics in my room. I will show you." Lady Lina kept looking at Matilda, as if she wanted to talk to her. Matilda knew her eyes would show the evidence of her recent tears, so she was not surprised.

Together the three women went through many fabrics that were in the trunk. "I have some silk, but it is in a color that would not look good with your skin tones. That is why it is still in my trunk. I do not think it would look good on anyone." Lady Lina kept digging. "Here. I think this will suit you nicely. It is a thin wool that would make a beautiful dress. How would you like to marry in green?"

Matilda had never had a choice of color of her clothing in her life. It was all fascinating to her. "I would be happy to wear whatever you think will look best on me, milady."

"This then," Lady Lina said, handing the fabric to Mary. "Can the two of you turn that into a dress fit for a wedding in two days?"

Mary nodded. "Aye, I am certain we can. Perhaps we could have some linen as well for new underthings."

Lina handed some linen cloth to Mary as well. It was white and would work perfectly for what Matilda needed.

As the two younger women started to leave, Lina stopped Matilda. "I would like to ask you a private question, if I may."

Matilda waited for Mary to shut the door behind her, which was not easy with her arms full of fabric, and then she turned her full attention to the woman who was about to be her mother-in-law. "Why do you cry?"

Matilda sighed. "We spoke to my parents, and they are happy with the marriage, but they are convinced we will never see each other again. Even Robert said that it would probably be best if I did not keep trying to see them. And they will not come for the wedding feast. They do not want to embarrass me."

"I see." Lady Lina sighed. "I am so sorry you are going through this. We do have a small cottage that is here on the property . . . well, there is a large house that is already furnished and waiting for Lord Alex and I to move into, and then there is a small cottage that sits empty. Would you parents like to move into it?"

Matilda's eyes grew wide. It had never occurred to her that this family would be generous to her parents as well as her. "I would love for them to move there, but I do not know if they will." She worried her parents' pride would keep them from wanting to take the house.

"I understand what you mean. I will send Alex and Robert to speak with them. I am certain that they can convince them to give up their lives of toil and hard work to be closer to you and the children you will soon be having. In fact," Lady Lina smiled. "I will tell the men to mention the children you will be having and say that you would feel better if your mother was close."

"You truly would not mind?"

"I would not mind at all. I would like to get to know them. They raised a lovely, intelligent young lady, so they must be good people." Lady Lina hugged Matilda. "I will do what I can to get them here before the wedding. If not, they will be here soon after. I am sure we can make that happen."

"Thank you, milady. It means a great deal to me to see you looking after my parents."

"Are you happy to be marrying Robert?" Lina asked softly.

Matilda nodded. "Yesterday, I was not so sure how I felt, but after our walk last night . . . aye, I am happy to be marrying Robert. I feel a little like I am being washed away by a great river, but I am happy to be marrying him."

Lina laughed. "Feeling like you are being washed away by a giant river is exactly how you should feel if you are marrying a man you met yesterday in two days. You will be fine. If you find you need anything else from me, let me know, but I am going to start working on my husband and son to talk to your parents, and I will start talking to the kitchen about the feast." She hurried out the door, only to stop at the top of the stairs to look back at Matilda. "Welcome to the family."

Matilda teared up at the words. "Thank you." She hurried into her room to start sewing with Mary, knowing the process would take a long time. She would not be wearing one of the simple dresses she would worn every day of her life. This would be an elaborate dress meant for the nobility.

Closing her door, she looked at Mary. "How can I help you?"

Mary looked at her. "We need to take measurements and figure out how much fabric to use. This is going to have to be done quickly. If you have a good hand with a needle, I will have you work on the undergarments."

"Aye, of course." Matilda stood in the middle of the room and let her friend measure the fabric against her, watching as she marked it in different places. "Now the real work begins."

Matilda and Mary worked the rest of the morning, until Robert knocked on the door. "It is time for the noon meal, and I want my bride beside me!"

Matilda and Mary exchanged smiles as Matilda hurried for the door. "I am coming. I do not want you to see what we have done with the wedding gown, though. I want you to be surprised."

Robert took her hand and led her toward the stairs. "I already know how beautiful you are. No dress could ever cover that."

She walked with him toward the table. "I will be very busy with wedding preparations for the next day or two. I do not know how much we will see each other."

"As long as I have you for meals and a short walk after supper, I will be pleased. I would like to carry you around with me at all times, but I know that is not acceptable. I will wait until after we are wed for that."

She grinned, walking to the table with him. She was amazed at how much more comfortable she was with him than she had been the day before. It was as if their walk the previous night had removed her hesitations about him, and she was ready to move on with their lives.

Once they were seated at the table, she looked at his mother, who was making a list on a piece of paper as they sat there. "Are you going to spend the entire meal scribbling, wife?" Lord Alex asked.

Lady Lina nodded. "I have to make a list of the foods we will serve at the wedding feast. That way the kitchen can be ready."

"Who exactly will come to this feast?" he asked. "We have not had time to send messages to anyone."

"All of the serfs who live on our land will be invited. Every single one of them. And we will have enough food to feed them all." Lina smiled at Matilda, who immediately understood. If all the serfs came, then her parents could come, too.

Matilda wanted to jump up and hug Robert's mother, but instead she sat quietly at the table, eating her meal. "I must hurry," she finally said. "Mary and I are going to be sewing nonstop until the wedding."

"I wish I could spare more of the maids to help with the dress, but it is going to take everyone we have just to get the cooking done." Lina shook her head. "Robert, can you give us a week? It would be so much easier if we could have more time."

Robert shook his head adamantly. "No, Mother. The wedding will be in two days. Even a week is too long to wait."

Lina sighed. "I was afraid you would say that. You are so much like your father!"

Robert reached over and squeezed Matilda's hand. "Why would any man agree to wait when he had such a beautiful woman at the end of his journey?"

Matilda noted that Robert had never said anything about being in love with her. He only talked about how beautiful she was. Did he have feelings other than lust for her? Or were they starting their marriage for all the wrong reasons? She had no idea, but she could not let it bother her either way. This wedding would give her parents an easier life as well as herself.

And truthfully at this point, she could not imagine not being married to Robert. He was the man she was meant to be with. She knew because he had told her so often. And she was just realizing that he was absolutely right.

As she went back upstairs and worked on her undergarments, she could not help but think about what a marriage without love would be? Her mother had always told her that love was for peasants, who only ever married for love. While the nobility had easier lives, they were often wed to people who they were horribly unhappy with.

She hoped that her marriage would be much more like a marriage of peasants than one of the nobility. She wanted days of love and nights of passion. Her life was about to change forever in just two days. Hopefully the changes would be all for the good. She would be giving birth to seven sons in her marriage, and knowing that was just a little frightening. She wanted her mother there for her own sanity as much as she wanted her there so she would have a better life.

When Mary came back from her own noon meal, the two women worked together, and Matilda often stood to have the dress tried on. She just wished she could get her worries of what the future would bring out of her head.

CHAPTER FIVE

Early the following morning, Matilda woke in her new bedchamber, very disoriented for a moment. Her entire life she had slept in one room, and suddenly she was in two new rooms in two days. It was very confusing.

After a moment, she sat up and swung her feet to the floor, surprised by how well she had slept in such a comfortable place. Her place to sleep was usually the floor of the one-room home she had shared with her parents. This chamber was filled with such luxury, it was hard to believe it was hers for the moment.

Just as she was sitting up, Mary quietly slipped into the room with her. "Are you ready to start your day?" her friend asked.

Matilda nodded, rubbing her eyes. "We have to finish the dress today."

"And your underthings. You cannot go into a marriage with the heir of the castle without having proper underthings."

"I have a feeling he cares very little for my underthings and instead cares a great deal about what is *under* the underthings."

Mary giggled slightly. "it is probably true." She moved to help Matilda dress for her day in a dress that Matilda had never seen. "I have seen the way he looks at you, and the man is most definitely smitten."

Matilda did not believe Robert was smitten even a little bit. "Where did you find it?"

"Lady Lina said it once belonged to her daughter, and she was hoping you would not mind her presumption in sending it to you."

Matilda looked down at the beautiful dress, which would have been worth everything she had ever worn put together. "I love it." She could not help but think about the fact that Lady Lina had a daughter, and she herself never would. Mayhap she and Robert could also find an orphaned child and raise her as their own.

"It looks like it was made for you." Mary stepped

back and studied Matilda for a moment. "Sit, and I will fix your hair."

Matilda found that Mary had become a great deal bossier since she was assigned as her maid, but there was no point in saying anything about it. A good maid was more of a partner than an inferior . . . at least that is what Lady Lina had told her.

When she walked down the stairs to break the fast, Matilda found Robert waiting for her. "You look beautiful this morning." He offered his arm and escorted her to the great hall. "Your chamber was comfortable?"

"Very. I am afraid I am not used to such luxury. Are you not worried I will come to expect to be treated like a lady?"

He laughed. "I expect others to treat you as a lady, and I hope you will come to love it. Of course, you will be kept busy having children for the next ten years or so."

She shook her head. "What if I am not able to have children? Some women are barren!" She could not help but worry about her own mother's trouble having children who lived.

"You will not be. I promise. There is something about my family that means seven sons born quickly. You will be fine." He walked her to the table and held her chair out for her. "Good morning, Mother. Good morning, Father."

"Good morning," his mother responded, looking at Matilda instead of Robert. "How are you this morning? Was the chamber to your liking?"

Matilda smiled. "The chamber was the most luxurious I have ever even imagined. Thank you for letting me stay there."

"You will have our chamber after the wedding tomorrow. My husband and I have already begun moving our things into the house across the property. We will still be close enough to visit and enjoy our grandchildren but far enough that you will feel you have privacy."

"You do not have to leave on my account. I would happily let you stay here forever."

Lady Lina smiled and nodded. "I know you would, child, and I do appreciate it. I feel like I need to follow the family tradition of moving to the other home, just as Alex's parents did many years ago."

Matilda knew there was no point in protesting more. This family was very set in their traditions. "How are the preparations for the feast?"

"They are coming along wonderfully! I have asked Alex to have several of his men ride around to talk to the serfs today. They will all know that tomorrow has been declared a day of merrymaking, and they are invited to a wedding here at the castle that will include a feast."

"It is most generous of you to invite all the serfs, Lady Lina."

"I know you want your parents here to see you wed. They will be, and the other serfs will be here to make them feel comfortable."

Matilda still worried that her parents would not come to the wedding, but she did not voice her thoughts. She was doing her best to remain positive and not overwhelmed by the entire situation—and most especially by the man beside her. "I thank you for your efforts."

Robert reached over and grasped her hand in his under the table, squeezing it tightly. "All will work out for the best."

She smiled slightly, forcing her attention to the food in front of her.

Once their meal was over, Robert led her to the bottom of the stairs. "I am forced to run around doing whatever I am told like a common lackey as Mother gets everything just so for the wedding tomorrow."

"At least we know it will not rain," she said softly.

He frowned. "How do we know that? We live in England, the land of rain."

She smiled at him with mischief in her eyes. "Your mother will not let it. She does control the weather after all."

He laughed. "She does. All right. I will take your word for the fact that there will be no rain on the morrow." He leaned down and brushed his lips across hers. "I hope you have a good morning, and I will see you at lunch. Now to go be a lackey . . ."

As he wandered off, she giggled a little. It was nice to see him humbled enough to do the errands his mother bid him to do.

Her morning passed pleasantly, chatting with Mary while they both sewed as quickly as their fingers allowed. She was pleased with the decision to have Mary as her personal maid. She knew it would make things easier for her, while she helped Mary. Both were good things in her opinion.

―――

Robert spent his entire morning riding all over his father's land, inviting different people to his wedding. He made sure he personally went to Matilda's parents, not wanting them to be afraid to attend the wedding. When he reached her father, the man's face was hard. It was astonishing to him how much older her parents looked than his, but they had lived much harder lives.

He swung down from his horse's back and walked over to her father. "It is good to see you again," he said, hoping the polite conversation would get the man talking.

Her father stopped working and stood looking at Robert. "I would have thought we would said everything there was to say yesterday."

Robert took a deep breath, realizing this discussion would be more difficult than he had realized. "I came to invite you to your daughter's wedding. Every serf on my father's land is invited and given a day away from work. It would mean a great deal to Matilda and myself if you came."

The man sighed. "She will not be pleased if we come. We are just a reminder that she did not start out life as privileged as she will end it."

"On the contrary, it means a great deal to her that you and your wife are both there. My mother has arranged a home where the both of you may live after the wedding as well. There will be no more work required of you. Her station will lift yours as well." Robert hoped the man would take his words the way they were meant. He badly wanted Matilda's wishes for her parents to come true.

Her father frowned. "I will discuss both with her mother."

"I beg you to come because you attending the wedding and living close to us would make my bride very happy. I do hope you will agree." Robert felt he must do all he could to get them to be a part of Matilda's life. Begging a serf had not ever been something he thought he would do, yet he found himself doing it with ease.

"I will think on it."

Robert knew there was nothing else he could say that would sway the man if his words had not already done so. "I will be off. The wedding is in the morn, just before the noon meal. There will be food for all." He assumed there would also be games and dancing, but there was no way to know. His mother had not given him a great deal of details about the party that would follow the ceremony. He trusted her to make it something he would be proud of.

He rode onto the next field and talked to the peasant who worked there, explaining about his wedding and the festivities that would follow. The only person he had spoken to so far who had not given a resounding aye was his future father-in-law. He hoped that was not a glimpse of what was to come for him and his sweet Matilda.

Matilda was surprised about her disappointment at the noon meal. Robert was still out riding around inviting people to their nuptials, and he had taken a meal with him to eat along the way. He was not going to be there to eat with her, and she felt very out of place sitting down with only her future mother and father-in-law. She had a great deal of respect for both, but she felt as if she was out of her league without Robert there. She actually missed him, which was rather astonishing.

Taking the spot where Robert usually had her sit, she tried to keep her head down, so she would not be noticed. She did not know why she was so certain his parents would be upset with her for being there, but there was no doubt in her mind they would.

"How comes the dress, Matilda?" Lady Lina asked with a smile.

Matilda looked over at her and shrugged. "I think we will be finished when we need to be. Mary is sewing as quickly as she can, and she has said she will work through the night if that is what it takes to finish."

Lady Lina nodded at the news. "I have the servants starting to roast meat for the party tomorrow. it will be a day-long event with dancing, games, and much merriment. You and Robert are only required to stay until after the evening meal, and then others will feel they can leave as you do."

"So no one can leave until Robert and I do?"

Lady Lina shook her head. "No, it is considered rude to leave before the bride and groom. No one would dare."

Matilda felt a bit more pressure laid on her shoulders with those words. She not only needed to learn all the rules of aristocratic etiquette, but she needed to worry about those rules. She was not looking forward to being the center of attention the following day. "How will I know what I am supposed to do?" she asked softly.

Lina looked at her for a moment, and then her eyes widened. "You will be fine, child. I will be there, and if you are slow to do something, I will come and whisper to you. Do not worry about that. You have the Lain family behind you now, and you have our love."

"Love?" Matilda asked, surprised by the word. Even Robert had not proclaimed love for her. She had no idea if that is what he felt or if it was just overwhelming lust, but either way, she was about to marry him.

"Aye, love. You will be one of our daughters." Lina smiled at her as she took a sip of her water.

"Hurry and eat so you can get back to sewing. We do not want you going to your own wedding tomorrow in a dress that was once our eldest's."

Matilda looked down at her dress, the most luxurious she had ever worn. "It would not be a hardship to wear this dress for anything, milady."

"No, it would not be. I hope after tomorrow, you will feel comfortable calling me Mother. We will have our things out before nightfall tonight and will only spend one last night here, and we will be in our new home tomorrow eve."

"I wish you did not feel the need to go." Truthfully, married or not, Matilda did not feel like she knew Robert well enough to live alone with him. She wished his parents would stay at least for a while.

"But we do, Matilda. You do not want your husband's parents living with you as you get used to married life. Trust me on this."

As soon as lunch was over, Matilda hurried up the stairs, feeling like she should stay and help with the dishes but knowing that it would be frowned upon. When she got into the room with Mary, she hurried to her bed and sat down, her eyes wild.

Mary stood up, dropping the gown she would been sewing. "Are you all right, Matilda? What is wrong?"

"I feel like I am swimming in a vast ocean with no help . . . and no ability to swim!"

"I am sure it all feels overwhelming," Mary said, sitting beside Matilda on the bed. "I would feel very lost in your shoes."

Matilda felt a tear course down her cheek. "I am not sure I am ready to be married to a nobleman . . . or any other man. I have known Robert for three days, and I am marrying him on the morrow! That is madness!"

Mary smiled, wrapping her arm around her friend's shoulders. "I think you will find it is the smartest thing you have ever done. Rumor has it that Lady Lina has arranged a cottage here on the castle grounds for your family. Does that please you?"

"It pleases me, and it would please me more if I knew my parents would agree to this thing. All I have heard from them is that I should move on with my life and forget them!" Matilda shook her head. "How could I ever forget the people who have meant the most to me in my life?"

Mary smiled. "I know how you are feeling. Truly I do. My parents will be coming to the wedding tomorrow, and I have not seen them since I came to work in the castle a few years back. I hope that it is not awkward between us."

Matilda nodded, not thinking of things from her

friend's point of view. She had given up her family, too, but simply for the servant's position she held with this family, not for a place in it. She took a deep breath. "I am acting like a small child, crying with fear of the unknown. I am a strong, capable woman. I can do this."

"I understand being afraid. You have known one thing your entire life, and now you are living in a new place, and you are about to be married to a strong nobleman. Robert is a very handsome man, but he is also very intimidating. I do not think I could be married to him."

"I did not think so either, but then he kissed me, and all the world changed. I can imagine being kissed by him every day for the rest of my life, however long it shall be."

Mary smiled. "So, he is a good kisser, is he?"

Matilda blushed, realizing just then that she would been running away at the mouth, saying things that should not have been said. "I think we should get back to our sewing."

"I think so as well." Mary could not keep the grin off her face as she moved across the chamber to a chair and resumed her sewing. "How are your nightgowns coming?"

For the rest of the afternoon, they talked about unimportant things, like sewing and Mary's work in the castle, but Matilda knew she had a confidante in her maid that she would have beside her for a long time to come. "I am glad it is you who will be my maid, Mary," Matilda said at the very end of the day, right before she tried on her wedding gown for the last time. It was almost perfect.

"I too, milady. We shall be lady and maid, but also friends. Should be a good situation for us both."

Matilda smiled as Mary helped her try on the dress and proclaimed it perfect. "I will be here right after the morning meal to help you dress and fix your hair. Would you prefer I brought your food on a tray?"

Matilda nodded. "That would be very nice. I do not know if I will be up to going to eat with his family in the morning because I am certain there will be an entire hive of hornets living in my belly."

"Most people just have butterflies . . ."

"I promise you, I will be the one who has hornets plaguing her!"

HER AFTER-SUPPER STROLL WITH ROBERT that evening was very uncomfortable for Matilda. She knew that the next time she saw him, she would be his in the eyes of God and England. His property to do with as he would. Of course as his serf she was already that, but being a wife was so much more.

"Did you talk to my parents today, milord?"

Robert wrapped his arm around her shoulders, pulling her close to his side as they walked. He could think of little else but that on the morrow she would be his forever, and he could finally stop restraining himself and touch her as he wanted. "I did. Your father has said they will consider your offer to come to the wedding and to come and live on the castle grounds."

"I am glad," she said simply. "I worry they will shut me out of their lives when there is truly no need to do so."

"No, there is not a need, and I was very clear with your father when I told him exactly that. I told him it would make you happy to have the two of them at our wedding and living so close."

"Thank you for doing that for me, Robert."

They reached the bench where he had kissed her for the first time, and he did not hesitate. He pulled her down onto his lap and kissed her passionately, his mouth opening hers and his tongue stroking inside insistently. "I cannot wait until you are mine!"

Matilda took a deep breath. "I am very nervous about becoming yours, milord. I came to the castle to be a maid just two days ago, and here I am, sitting atop you, planning to marry you in the morning. How did this happen?"

He smiled. "Mother used to call me a hurricane. She said it was the only type of storm that was even close to the damage I could cause!"

"Damage?" His words made no sense to her.

"Just like my mother's emotions are tied to her powers, so are mine. If she becomes angry a wild storm blows up. If I become angry, objects begin to swirl around me, and sometimes those objects hit people."

Matilda tilted her head to one side. "You will not be getting angry with me, will you, milord?"

"I certainly hope not. I care about you and plan to cherish you for all of my days. If I could wrap you in fine cotton to keep you safe, I would do just that."

Matilda rested her head on his shoulder, pleased with his words. "I will try hard not to be nervous about being wed to you then."

"Are you nervous of being the center of attention or of the wedding night?" he asked.

"More the wedding night, I am afraid. I have never even been alone with a man before you. How will I handle being so intimate with you?"

Robert looked into her eyes for a moment, and then he looked around to be certain no one was watching them. "I will do my best to calm your fears." With those words, he leaned down and pressed his lips to hers once again. His hand came up and rested on the side of her breast, while the other kept her in his lap by keeping a firm pressure at the back of her waist.

Matilda wrapped her arms around him and kissed him back for all she was worth. Never had she felt such sensations. When his hand moved around to cup her breast through her clothes, she moaned softly, her hands tangling in his hair.

Robert broke his mouth from hers, panting heavily. "How do you feel now, Matilda?"

"There is an ache inside me . . ."

"That ache will only feel better once we have had our wedding night. I promise you that ache will be fulfilled as quickly as I possibly can." He rested his forehead against hers. "Our wedding night will make us both happy. I promise you this."

She sighed. "I will endeavor to stop worrying then, milord." She sat where she was for a moment, and then she got to her feet. "We should go back to the castle. We have a very busy day ahead of us tomorrow, and I think we both need as much sleep as possible."

"I do not know about you, but I will spend my night lying awake, staring at the ceiling, reliving that kiss, and remembering what it felt like to hold you in my arms and hear you moan with pleasure from what I was doing to you."

Matilda gasped at his words, happy no one was around to hear them. "You will look tired on our wedding day, then."

He laughed. "I will. But it does not matter. You will be mine whether I am tired or not."

CHAPTER SIX

Matilda woke with a start the next morning. Her night had been a fitful font of dreams of Robert, his head hovering above hers, his lips upon her own. She sat up in her bed and hugged her knees to her chest. It was her last morning waking up alone. Her wedding day.

Mary swept in as Matilda put her feet on the floor, a tray of food in her hand. "I am not sure I can eat for the hornets buzzing around in my middle." Matilda had never been so very nervous about something in her life. She had to be able to push through this and marry Robert.

Mary set the tray on a small table across the room from Matilda's bed and poured two glasses of water. "it is your wedding day, Matilda! It is time for rejoicing, not hiding under your covers in fear of the unknown. Come! I am breaking the fast with you this morning."

Mary's chipper attitude did little to make Matilda feel better. "I am making a mistake. I just know I am."

"You are not. You are changing your destiny. Your children will not toil in the fields as we both did as babes. Your children will be raised in this castle, and they will be the future lords and ladies, served here by those who you had thought to work the rest of your life with. It is time for you to shine, Matilda, and I am not going to let you hold yourself back." Mary gestured to the table where their meal was waiting. "Eat, and after you finish, you are going to have a bath, and I am going to wash your hair."

"Wash my hair? I hope you know I am perfectly capable of washing my own hair, Mary."

Mary grinned. "I do know you are. I hope you know that I am your maid, and it is now my job to take care of your hair."

"Aye, of course." Matilda sighed. "I am nervous. I am nervous about marrying, and I am nervous about seeing my parents when I do not know how they feel about this wedding. Everything is making me nervous today. Mayhap I really should get back under those covers." Waking again in a better frame of mind seemed to be the answer.

Mary simply laughed. "Come and eat with me. You will feel better after a good meal." She took her seat and picked up her spoon. "it is delicious."

Matilda sat down across from her friend. "I am not sure I am up to eating."

"Well, then I will eat my share *and* your share. You have not been walking through this castle. The meats have been roasting since yesterday afternoon, and I promise you, as soon as you step foot out of this chamber, the aromas will assault your senses, and you will be able to think of nothing but the food you will have later. When Lady Lina said she was inviting every peasant in the land, she meant it. There is more meat roasting than I have ever seen at one time. There will be enough to feed all of the land and France as well!"

Matilda smiled at that, taking a bite of her good. "Are you trying to help me with my nervousness or is that just happening by chance?" Having a friend beside her was helping tremendously. How could she stay in a bad mood when the girl beside her was so chipper?

Mary laughed. "Robert stopped me on my way up the stairs, and he promised me that I would be his favorite maid if I would make sure you made it down to the chapel for your wedding. He is afraid you will get cold feet."

"He knows me better than I think he does."

"In all the time I have been working here, I have never seen Lord Robert become interested in anyone, maid or lady. The moment he saw you, he was convinced you were meant to be together. That tells me that you are the one he has been waiting his entire life for. I hope you make him as happy as he thinks you will."

Matilda had not considered once whether she was the right woman to make Robert happy, only worrying if he was the right man to make her happy. Instantly she felt regret, as if she had acted like a spoiled child. She promised herself there and then that she would do her utmost to make her future husband happy. It was her duty as a wife, after all.

After she broke the fast, Matilda hid behind the changing screens across the room and waited as several of the male servants came in one after the other with buckets of hot water to fill her bath. After Mary closed the door, Matilda came out from behind the screen and sank into the tub.

Her family had not had the luxury of an actual bathtub, and instead they had bathed with a cloth and water whenever they could. She could not believe just how good it felt to sink into the water up to her shoulders, and she sighed with pleasure as she did so. "I want to take a bath every morning, Mary."

Mary laughed. "I can arrange that for you if it is what you would really like."

"Really?" Matilda had thought she was asking for something absolutely outrageous, but Mary took it in stride.

"Absolutely. Lady Lina bathes every night after supper. No one expects anything different from her."

"Would that not make me seem as though I was trying to act above my station?" Matilda asked in confusion. She truly worried that the servants would think less of her because they knew she would once been one of them. The whole situation was difficult for her.

"I do not think you understand the love the entire household has for this family, Matilda. We all love and want to serve the people who live here. It is not a matter of duty even. It is simply that we all have great feelings of thankfulness for them. For the way we are treated."

"I have never heard of a family in the nobility treating their people well. My father has always talked about how cruel the privileged nobility can be. He lived here before the current family, though, and they were not nearly as kind to the peasants."

"This family treats every servant as they would a

member of their own family. I do not think you really understand how kind they truly are. If they see a peasant ill, they are often brought to the castle so Lady Lina can heal them. It is an amazing family you are marrying into. I think you will be very happy, and I know you will make Robert happy just by smiling at him every morning."

Matilda took a deep breath. She had been so focused on herself and her parents since she would come to the castle. Today, she would give herself for the rest of her life to Lord Robert, and she would learn to be the best wife she could be . . . but even more than that, she would make sure she learned the ways of the nobility, so she would never embarrass him.

After her hair was washed, Matilda sat still while Mary combed it dry. Matilda could not believe all the new experiences she was having, and she had never once expressed gratitude to the man who was changing her life. Instead she had argued with him and demanded that he try to get her parents there for the wedding. Surely, he must think her the most ungrateful woman alive.

Mary talked to her softly as she brushed her hair, and Matilda felt tingles up and down her spine. It felt good to have someone care for her in such a way.

It did not take long for Matilda to fall asleep as

Mary brushed her hair over and over, and she was startled to be woken. "Your hair is dry. it is time to get you dressed for your wedding, milady."

"How long did I sleep?" Matilda asked groggily.

"No more than an hour." Mary took the dress she would made off a hook it had been hanging from and held it in front of her. "You will look so beautiful today. No one will have any doubts why Lord Robert would marry a maid in his mother's castle."

"I care nothing about how anyone views me but Robert himself. I do hope he will be pleased with me, though." Matilda hoped she would see her parents before the wedding, but after would be soon enough. It was a strange situation for her, but it would be so much better if her parents relented and were willing to be beside her.

After she was clothed, she sat in the same chair where she had fallen asleep a short while before, while Mary worked her magic on her hair. "Robert liked how you fixed my hair yesterday," Matilda told her maid. "He commented on how lovely I looked."

"That was a hairstyle for every day. I want you to look like you are a lady when you marry your lord. You will look your absolute best for this wedding. I promise you that."

"I know you will do all you can," Matilda said with a smile.

There was a knock on the door, and Mary hurried over and cracked the door just a bit to see who stood there. "Lady Lina!"

Lina stepped in and sat down on the edge of Matilda's bed, surprising the younger woman with her casual actions. "You look lovely. Robert is pacing a rut into the stone of the parlor as he works out his nervous energy. I expect objects to go flying any moment."

Matilda smiled. "He hasn't acted nervous, and he is constantly trying to still my nerves."

"I think he is worried about whether or not your parents will come. They would not promise, but I do know he tried his hardest."

Matilda took a deep breath and smiled at her future mother-in-law. "I would like them here, but what really matters is that Robert and I go before the priest and say our vows." Robert would do anything for her, and she needed to repay that by doing what he so desperately wanted—marrying him with a smile.

Lina grinned. "You are very right." She pulled a small package from behind her back and held it out for Matilda to see. "I have a gift for you. It is a pair of hair combs that I have had for a very long time. I think they would look lovely on you." She walked over to hand the combs to Matilda, who looked down at them.

"Oh, they are beautiful, milady. I would be honored to wear them."

Lina leaned down and hugged Matilda tightly. "Welcome to the family, my daughter. And please, make my son happy. I cannot wait to hold the sons you will bear." With those words, Lina was gone, and Matilda was left staring at the closed door.

Mary reached down and took the combs from Matilda. "They are truly beautiful. There are pearls on them . . ."

"I will feel as if I have the crown jewels in my hair for my wedding. Mayhap I should put them somewhere safe, so I can return them to her . . ." Matilda could not imagine a worse way to start a marriage than losing her mother-in-law's precious hair jewels.

"Did not you hear her say they were a gift? No, you will wear them on your wedding day. They will go beautifully with your hair."

Matilda's hair had never been cut. Her mother had always insisted that her beauty was magnified by her hair. It had been a nuisance most of the time, but her mother had promised her that when she married, it would cease to be a problem. Instead she would be happy it was long and beautiful. "As you wish. If I lose them, you will only have yourself to blame, though."

"You will not lose them. It is not like you are going to be running about the castle grounds today. You will be followed everywhere you go. I doubt if Lord Robert will allow you out of his sight."

"Is it bad that I am happy he is nervous as well? I want him to be as nervous as I am about this wedding."

"He is probably just nervous he will accidentally make people fly about during the service in his nervousness."

Matilda giggled. "Does everyone know about his powers?"

"Most of the castle servants do, but none of us will ever say a thing. Mayhap that is the reason the family is so wonderful to us, so we will keep their secrets. Between Lord Robert's making things fly about, and Lady Lina causing storms inside the castle, there are many things that would frighten people."

"They are Christian, are they not?" Matilda could not believe she would never thought to ask the question before.

"Aye, they are, and they are good Christians. Lady Lina always wears a cross around her neck, and you will find that Lord Robert has a cross on his armor as well as another at the hilt of his sword."

Matilda nodded, knowing that the family was not evil. Surely, she would know if they were. The servants would be afraid of them and not nearly so loyal.

When Mary finished with her hair, Matilda walked over to the window overlooking the yard below. It was completely swarmed with peasants, and Matilda's eyes searched through the crowd, hoping against hope to find her parents. Suddenly she let out a gasp. "I see them! They came!"

Mary hurried to the window with her. "Your parents?"

"Aye, see? They are just past the portcullis. Can you see them?"

Mary looked to see if she could tell who Matilda was speaking of, but she gasped instead. "I see my parents as well!"

Matilda turned to Mary and hugged her close. "Please say a prayer that Mother and Father will stay in the cottage that Lady Lina has offered them. I need them close." Being married to Robert and having her parents living close by where they could help as needed . . . well, it almost seemed like heaven on earth at that moment.

"I think having them here for the wedding means

that they are willing to stay. Will you try to talk to them today?"

"Absolutely, if I can find a way." Still watching, she smiled as she saw Robert bow before her father, his arms waving with wide gestures. A moment later, her parents were following him. "I believe Robert has convinced my parents to accompany him into the castle. This is good!"

Mary smiled as she watched Matilda's face rather than the scene unfolding below. The sheer joy on her face made her seem to almost glow with pleasure.

Within moments, there was a knock at the door, and Mary hurried to open it. "Aye?" she called as she opened it just far enough to see who was there.

"You know that Matilda has been eager to see her parents. Let us in so they may speak to her before the wedding," Lord Robert said.

"No, sir. I will let them in, but you are not going to see Matilda until the wedding. Go away, milord."

Matilda put her hand over her mouth, surprised at the way Mary chased her betrothed away. It amused her to see a loyal servant treat one of the children of the castle that way—especially since it was one who would be the master the following day.

The door opened then, and her parents stepped into her chamber, looking wary. Matilda rushed to her mother, embracing her immediately. "I am so glad you came! Will you stay in the cottage?"

Her mother sighed, looking into her face. "What would we do? We have worked all our lives, child."

"And that is why you should not have to work now. Move into the cottage, and if you want, I am sure Robert will see that you have jobs to do around the castle. Mostly, I just want you both here." Matilda took her mother's hand and led her to the bed where they both sat. "Robert is the seventh son of a seventh son. The family has had generation after generation with seven sons. I want my mother to be close while I go through pregnancy and childbirth. I want my children to know all of their grandparents. Please."

Her mother frowned at her for a moment and then nodded. "I never could tell you no, could I?"

"I am so glad." Matilda buried her face in her mother's shoulder, so happy she was there.

There was another knock on the door, and a loud voice called, "It is Lady Lina!" Mary hurried to the door and opened it. "The wedding is to start in a short while. Is your father to walk you to Robert?"

Matilda turned her attention to her father, who shook his head. "No, I will not. I will be there, though, and we will proudly watch you marry your man."

Matilda started to argue, but she knew with the way her father was dressed, he would not feel comfortable walking by her side to the priest. "It is fine. I can walk alone. I am just happy that you are here and you will stay."

Lady Lina smiled, clapping her hands together. "You will stay? The cottage was readied, and we were hopeful, but we were not certain. I am so pleased to meet you."

Matilda realized then she needed to introduce her parents to her future mother-in-law. "Lady Lina, may I introduce my parents, John and Esther? Mother and Father, this is Robert's mother, Lady Lina."

"Please just call me Lina. We will be grandparents of the same beautiful boys after all." Lina smiled at her mother, who smiled back tentatively. She seemed very nervous to be addressed by a lady.

"It is good to meet you," Esther said. "Thank you for taking care of our daughter in our absence."

"Matilda is already a member of the family." Lina walked over and took Matilda's hand. "I am going to lead your parents, and the rest of your wedding guests, into the chapel. After you see that all have disappeared, you may walk down to join us with Mary."

Matilda nodded, looking over at Mary, who had a serene smile on her face. "Aye, milady," Mary said.

After the others were gone, Matilda looked over at Mary. "Please tell me one more time that I am doing the right thing. All these people are here for my wedding to a man I just met three days past. What am I thinking?" She knew her emotions were rapidly changing, and she felt as if she was losing her mind. One minute she was determined to be the best wife she could possibly be for Robert, and then next she was questioning whether she should marry him at all.

"You are definitely making the right choice, Matilda. For you, your parents, and for me as well. And for Robert, who has never been happier than he has since your arrival. You *must* marry him."

The two women watched together as the others hurried away from their view, and once the courtyard was cleared, Mary smiled. "It is time."

"I can do this, right?"

Mary chuckled softly, linking her arm with Matilda's. "You can do this in a way no other can. In a few hours, you will be mistress of this castle, and you will love it. All the servants are excited to help you learn."

"They do not hate me for trying to rise above my station?"

"Not at all. We are all happy for you. We talked about it in the kitchen just this morning."

Matilda frowned. "It just occurred to me that while all the other peasants on the land get the day off, the people who work here have to work harder than usual. It is not fair!"

"No one begrudges it. Give them time off if you can or slip them an extra coin for Christmas. All will be happy with that."

"I will talk to Robert about it soon." It was late summer, far from Christmas, but she was certain Robert would approve of her plan. She could not believe she had not thought of the extra work for the castle servants.

As the two of them walked down the stairs and toward the front door, Matilda realized the entire staff of the house was lined up between her and the entrance to the castle. Many of them said kind things as they passed and finally, when she reached the front door, the last person there was Alice, who had welcomed her to the castle kindly when she still felt weepy from leaving her mother.

"Proud of you, girl. We all are. Make our lord happy."

The words were simple, but Matilda felt herself tearing up. "I will do my best." Matilda smiled at the older woman, touching her arm gently as she walked past.

Mary smiled. "I hope you know they decided to do that to show honor to you."

Matilda sniffled. "I do not deserve it, but I am so happy they do not hate me."

"They all feel like they can do more in their lives because of what you have done here. No one hates you. We all respect you. Me most of all because you have changed my life with your own."

"Thank you for being at my side." They had reached the chapel, and Matilda put her hand over her chest to keep from panicking. She forced her breathing to be even. "It is really time, is not it, Mary?"

"It is!"

"Can we just take a moment here? Before we go in and my life changes forever?"

"But your life is changing for the good, not the bad. Remember that as you are walking toward Lord Robert, Matilda. Your groom is a wonderful man, and your future mother-in-law already loves you. How can you not want to walk in that door?"

Matilda smiled and stood straighter, her shoulders back. She was going to marry Robert, who treated her as if she was a lady, not a maid. How *could* she not want to do that?

CHAPTER SEVEN

Matilda felt every eye on her as she walked between the two large groups of people toward the front of the church and her future husband. Robert stood at the front of the church, smiling at her proudly.

As soon as they were inside, Mary stopped walking beside her and blended in with the others around her. As she walked, she thought of all the reasons marrying Robert was not the best idea in the world, and then she passed her parents. Her mother was watching her with wide eyes, a tear on her face.

Her parents' lives would forever be changed by what she was about to do. How could she not marry the man who stood beside the priest? She lifted her chin a little bit more, and she finished the long walk, stopping beside Robert.

He held his hand out for hers, and she slipped her hand into it. After that, the service was held in Latin, and she stood and knelt as she was instructed to do. When the priest told them they were married, Robert grabbed her and kissed her. He looked down into her eyes, obviously pleased that they had made it that far.

"Let us go and feast with the serfs, my lady."

She smiled. "My parents are going to live in the cottage."

"I heard, and it thrills me beyond belief. And do you know why I will be so happy to live with your parents so very close to us? Most men would not be thrilled, you know."

"Why are you happy about it then?"

"Because it makes my new wife happy. Anything that brings a smile to your face pleases me." He hoped she realized just how strong his feelings for her were. He knew she was the woman put on the earth just to be his bride.

Matilda took his arm, and the two of them walked through the large crowd of people, all there to wish them well. Well, that was not fair. Matilda knew as well as everyone else that most of them were not there to wish her well. Instead they were there to get free food and not have to toil in the fields. It sounded like a good reason to be there to her!

Many people stopped her and Robert as they walked through the crowds. Some were peasants simply wanting to tell their lord how their crops were. One man stopped them to tell him that the wedding would be the highlight of his entire life. "I never dreamed I would be invited to a wedding for my lord. Thank you!" He bowed his head, and his toothless wife smiled beside him.

When they had finally reached the back of the church, his parents were waiting for them. Robert smiled at his mother. "Now you get to take over everything, and we are nothing but simple party-goers for the rest of the day, correct?"

"Oh, absolutely! You two need to mingle and talk to people if you would like, but mostly you need to be together." His mother pulled his head down and kissed his cheek. "My seventh son has finally found his bride, and I could not be happier."

"I am sorry I did not give you time to get your other sons and your daughter here as well."

"I am not. You did a good job, and I am so pleased with your bride." Lady Lina hugged Matilda, kissing her cheek as well. "Welcome to the family."

Matilda smiled in return. "I believe that is the

third time you have welcomed me to the family, Lady Lina. I thank you."

"Please, call me Mother, as Robert does."

Matilda nodded. "Thank you, Mother."

Robert's arm stayed locked around Matilda's waist as the day progressed. After just picking at her meal, Matilda found she was truly hungry. She and Robert shared a trencher at the head of the table at lunch. There were people all around the table, and more tables and benches had been put out in the courtyard. The peasants would eat in shifts, but they would all be able to partake of the feast offered to them there.

At one point, Matilda saw a spoon float off the table, but she quickly caught it and lowered it before anyone noticed. "Your happiness is showing, milord," she whispered into his ear.

"How could it not?" He smiled at her, obviously thrilled that she was finally his. "I have waited for the day I would marry the woman who was created just for me for my entire life. Now that day is here, and I cannot stop smiling."

When the feast was over, there was dancing. Matilda was surprised to see that there were several servants who were still roasting meat, until she remembered that the party would go on through supper time. They would all need to be fed again.

A man held a lute and sang while standing atop a platform. As soon as the music started, Robert took Matilda's hand and led her in a simple dance. She hissed at him that she had never danced before, but he made sure to move slowly so she could easily follow his footsteps. It was his wedding day, and Robert was going to dance with his bride. It was as simple as that.

At the end of the dance, they were both laughing, and many others joined for the next song.

Through the whole long day of feasting, Matilda stayed close to Robert, and he kept a hand on her arm or an arm around her. Never did they lose contact even once.

They both took time to walk among the peasants and talk to them of whatever was on their minds. Matilda felt her feelings for Robert grow stronger as she watched him give his full attention to each of the people he talked to throughout the long day. She knew he wanted nothing more than to carry her up the stairs to their chamber and spend the day there with her, but he never let on to other people. They all truly believed that he wanted nothing more than to stand there and talk to them. It was a great skill to have for a man in his position.

Matilda stayed quiet and listened as he talked about everything anyone wanted to discuss. There was no nobility there other than his family. It was all peasants, so her parents would feel comfortable there. She was amazed at the sacrifices his family had made for *her* comfort.

At supper at the end of the night, there were very few people invited to dine with her and Robert. The table consisted of Matilda, her parents, Robert, and his parents. "it is probably wrong to admit it, but I am pleased that it is just us at supper this evening. The constant crush of people was getting overwhelming," Matilda said softly.

Robert smiled. "That is why Mother arranged this. She was certain you would need a little time away from the big crowd."

"The lute player is very good. I have enjoyed his music."

Lady Lina smiled at her. "He is our horse trainer. He enjoys playing his lute every chance he gets. He has played for all eight of my children's weddings."

Matilda's mother turned to Lady Lina. "Matilda said everyone in your family had seven sons." She seemed confused about the eight weddings.

"I did have seven sons, but my husband and I took in a girl he found at the side of the road just before we met. Her family had been killed by fever, and she was brought to me to heal because I have knowledge of herbs and potions." Lady Lina did not tell the rest of the story, not sure if her parents were ready to know just what her family was like.

"I see. So if Matilda and Robert choose to take in a girl child, they are allowed to do so?" Esther seemed quite pleased with the possibility.

"Aye, of course. Matilda will give birth to seven sons, but they may raise any girls they wish."

Matilda smiled at her mother, covering her hand with hers. "You will have many grandchildren. They will just be boys." She wished it would be different because she had always had a special relationship with her mother, and she would like to share that relationship with a daughter.

Her mother smiled at her, a smile that looked almost sad. "I will be pleased to have grandchildren, but I must also be allowed to work. I cannot sit idle simply because my daughter has married a wealthy man."

Matilda frowned. "I wish you could. I would love your help with the children once they begin to come. Perhaps you could be their nurse and help me raise them."

Her mother grinned at the prospect. "That sounds like a wonderful idea. What shall I do in the meantime?"

Matilda looked at Lina, having no idea what positions needed to be filled in the castle or even what her mother should do. Lina saw the look and stepped in gracefully. "Matilda needs more clothes. Clothes that fit her new station in life. Currently she has the dress she is wearing and a dress my eldest once wore. If you are handy with a needle, Matilda's maid needs some help getting all the sewing done as quickly as possible."

Esther nodded, smiling. "I am very handy with a needle. I am not sure I can sew something as fancy as what she is wearing, but I can learn."

"Matilda's maid is very good with fancy clothes. Perhaps you could make her nightgowns. Then Mary can show you what needs to be sewn in the gowns."

"That sounds wonderful. I would love to help my daughter and earn my keep at the same time." Esther grinned at her husband, who nodded to her. "And my husband? What can he do?"

"Flowers," Matilda blurted out. "I find the castle grounds sadly lacking in flowers. I believe father can grow anything under any circumstances. He could plant and grow flowers."

Lady Lina smiled. "He can help the groundskeeper. It sounds like it would be the perfect occupation for him."

Matilda looked over at her mother. "See, Mama? I knew we would find something to keep you quite busy."

"As long as your offer still stands to help you take care of grandbabies when they come, I will be happy forever," Esther said.

"Oh, I would not be able to do it without you!" Matilda knew there were many women she could hire to help her with her future sons, but none she would trust as she trusted her mother. She could not recall even once her mother had raised her voice to her. Why, she was practically a *saint* with children!

After supper, Robert pulled Matilda out to dance with her one more time. After their dance, he whispered in her ear, "I do believe it is time for people to be able to go home, and that means we must bid them goodnight." He tried to keep the eagerness from his voice, but he was unsure if he was successful.

"What about my parents? Who will help them find the cottage?"

"My mother will help them. You cannot put this off any longer, Matilda. It is time."

Matilda nodded, realizing he was right. He and his family had already done a great deal for her to make her happy. She could not begrudge him his wedding night, no matter how nervous the prospect made her. "Aye, milord."

"You may use my name," he said in an almost growl in her ear.

She giggled. "I will try to remember . . . milord." She did not know why she persisted in teasing him, but it amused her a great deal.

He shook his head at her, a grin on his face. As soon as the song was over, he put his hands at Matilda's waist and lifted her onto the platform with the lute player before climbing up behind her. He put his arm around her waist and raised his hand for attention. When all was quiet, he said loudly, "My wife and I would like to thank you for attending our wedding and making our joy your joy. I hope you will all celebrate with us as we have many children through the years. God bless you all!"

Matilda turned to him and smiled, stepping closer to Robert and pulling his head down for a kiss. She knew the crowd would love to see her as the aggressor in a kiss, and she was right. The cheers that came from the peasants watching had her laughing softly as she pulled away. "I thought that would please them."

Robert shook his head at her, loving the look of mischief in her eyes. "You will always keep me on my toes, will not you, Matilda?"

"I will not let you grow bored in our marriage," she said by way of answering him. Her impish grin had him wondering if he knew his new bride as well as he thought he did.

Getting down, Robert lifted her down after him, and they walked toward the entrance to the castle. His mother stood there, waiting for them. "All of your things have been moved into the chamber you will now share with Robert," she told Matilda. "I will send Robert up in a few minutes after you have had some time to get undressed and ready yourself for bed."

Robert frowned at his mother. "I can help her undress!"

"Her maid will do it."

Matilda smiled at Lina and rushed toward the stairs, wondering how on earth she was going to find Mary with the big crowd of people outside the castle. When she got to her room, her maid was waiting for her. "Lady Lina sent me up here right after supper. She said Robert was going to do well to wait for just one dance to be over before he dragged you up here."

Matilda blushed, but she presented her back to Mary to help her undress. "I appreciate you waiting here for me. We must hurry because it was all Lady Lina could do to keep Robert from following me up immediately."

Mary nodded and helped her push the gown off her shoulders. "You have won the hearts of every nobleman, servant, and peasant at this wedding. Your attention to Robert and your lack of need to have all of his attention on you has not gone unnoticed. All are excited that you will be the new mistress here."

Matilda frowned. "Really? I just did what I thought was right."

"You will not have a problem with the servants or peasants here, Matilda. As soon as you realize that your husband loves you beyond belief, you are going to be very happy."

Matilda smiled, slipping between the sheets with nothing on, as custom demanded. She hoped there would not be a bedding ceremony as she had seen many times, but she had no idea what was planned.

Mary slipped from the room, and the door opened not a minute later. Robert walked to the side of the bed and methodically stripped off his clothing. He had only one thing on his mind, and that was his bride, lying naked under the covers of their bed. The bed where their children would be conceived, and where they would later be born. The bed where he would spend the rest of his nights sleeping with the wife that he already treasured more than he had ever believed was possible. His bride.

He walked over and got into the bed, getting under the covers on the other side of the bed. His hand stroked down her arm, and he smiled at her.

"Are you ready to be my wife in more than just name?"

Matilda turned onto her side facing him. "I just realized that my name is Matilda Lain now. It sounds odd, does not it?"

"It sounds wonderful and right." He leaned over and pressed a kiss against her lips. "I cannot believe we finally made it through this day. I thought it would never end."

She laughed. "I enjoyed myself. Thank you for teaching me to dance. And thank you for making my parents feel like they are an important part of both of our lives."

"It is my job to make you happy, and if it makes you happy to have your parents here, then I am pleased to do it." His hand slid under the cover, and he stroked her from arm to the tips of her fingers, bringing her hand to his lips. "I have always known I would find a woman who would then become the center of my world and who would bear me seven sons. I never dreamed she would be as beautiful as you are."

"Or that she would be a maid you found dusting the parlor?" Matilda could not resist teasing him about how he had first seen her.

"Is that what you were doing when I found you? I

thought you were gossiping about how strange I was."

"Well, there was that as well, milord." She leaned forward and pressed her lips to his, loving his kisses. She felt like she was complete and whole when his lips were on hers, and when he was not there she was bereft.

He rolled her to her back, his hand stroking over her belly and cupping her breast. "I plan to spend forever with you, Matilda."

"Show me how forever feels, milord."

He growled deep in his throat. "You only call me that to see if you can make me crazed!"

Matilda laughed, and her laughter felt good to her. She had not laughed as much in her entire life as she had since she met him. How had God decided to favor her with a man to spend the rest of her life with? Loving him as she was beginning to love this man. "Can I make you crazed, milord?"

He closed his eyes, and the covers floated off their bodies and onto the floor. "Now you have done it!"

She laughed. "I am worried I will grow cold! You should bring the covers back!"

"Not until I have warmed you through and through."

It was a long while later that they both lay on

their backs, breathing heavily. "I think I liked doing that with you, milord," Matilda said with her voice full of wonder.

"You *think?* I will have to try harder next time!" He gathered her to him and cradled her against his body, bringing the blankets back up from the floor to land over them both.

"Good night. Dream of me." Matilda was surprised at how bold she was being after what they had just done together. It was very unlike her, but this man brought out new things in her all the time.

"I have dreamed of nothing else since the moment we met." He closed his eyes and inhaled of her fragrance, thrilled that she felt so good against him. He was where he needed to be.

CHAPTER EIGHT

Matilda was nervous about taking control of the castle and commanding the servants. It seemed so odd to her that it was now her duty, but it was. Robert had returned to training his men, so she needed to face the servants. After spending a full day lazing about in the castle, it was time that they both returned to work.

It was two days after their marriage, and her mother and Mary were waiting in the chamber she had used before her wedding. They were patiently sewing, trying to get Matilda's clothing to reflect her station in life and not make everyone automatically know she would been a peasant.

She joined the two of them and discussed the type of gown she wanted first. They had both been working on undergarments and nightgowns until she came to them and described what she wanted.

Her mother looked her up and down, obviously trying to see if she was happy. "He treats you well?"

Matilda nodded, feeling the heat rise to her face. "He has shown me nothing but kindness, Mama. There is no need to worry about me." She sat down on the bed, curling one leg under her. "How is the cottage? Is it to your liking?"

"It is the most wonderful home. There is a bedroom separate from the rest of the house, and there is even a stove to cook on, instead of just the fireplace. I have never dreamed of living in such luxury."

Matilda smiled at her mother's words, knowing that she would felt the same way just days before. "I am so glad. Lady Lina told me it would be a good place for you and Father, but I have yet to see it."

Mary went to the trunk that held all of the fabrics that were there to choose from for Matilda's wardrobe. The three women chose a fabric and a dress style together. Then Mary went to Matilda's new room with her. She could not run around the castle all day in just her nightgown.

Matilda once again wore the dress that had once belonged to Robert's sister, and then she turned to Mary. "I am not sure what the servants expect from me. What am I supposed to do?" Facing them as their mistress instead of as an equal or even an inferior was intimidating for her.

Mary smiled. "The servants here are all well-trained. They know their duties. You simply need to go to the kitchen and discuss what you would like to have for meals with Alice, and she will handle the rest. There is really not a lot you will need to do before your sons start to come, and then you will always be busy with babies."

Matilda sighed. "I suppose I can take advantage of the time I have and read. There are a few books here, and I would love to read them."

"Sounds good, milady."

Matilda wrinkled her nose. "I am still Matilda to you, Mary. My wedding hasn't changed *our* relationship at all."

Mary grinned at her. "I will call you Matilda when we are alone, but I cannot do that with others around."

"I suppose that will have to be good enough, will not it?" Matilda left the room and descended the stairs. She had skipped eating that morning because

Robert had kept her up most of the night, and she had felt the need to sleep late instead of beginning her new life. No one seemed to think less of her for it.

She walked to the kitchen, and everyone stopped working, turning to her. "I just wanted to discuss meals for the week with Alice," she said softly. She was unsure why her presence was making everyone uncomfortable when just days before she had been one of them.

The servants all returned to their activities, and Alice took her arm and led her to the dining room. "This is a better place to discuss such things than the kitchen, milady."

Matilda frowned. "I have been in the kitchen with you several times, Alice. I am sure it is all right." Why did someone act as if she was a different person now just because she had married Robert?

Alice shook her head. "I am sure it is not. You are the lady of the house now."

Matilda sighed. "I am afraid I will never learn all the rules and behave the way I am expected to behave. I am not quite sure how I can adjust with no one here to teach me."

Alice smiled and sat down at the table, indicating that Matilda should sit down as well. "Before Lady Lina left, she suggested that I should be the one to teach you how to run a household. I have worked at this castle since your husband was a few months old, and I know what I am doing better than anyone. We will work together."

"That sounds wonderful! Are you sure you have the time to spare?"

"I am positive. Together, we are going to make sure everything runs smoothly around here." Alice smiled. "You are going to be the very best mistress this castle could ever have."

Matilda smiled and nodded. She was relieved that Lady Lina had given someone instructions to help her because she was truly afraid of messing up.

———

At the noon meal, Matilda realized that she would really missed her new husband. He would become such a huge part of her life that when he was not there for a few hours, it felt as if there was a huge gaping hole in the middle of her being. When he came to join her in the great hall, she went into his arms sweetly and kissed him. "How was your morning?" She clung to him a little longer than normal and wished she could express her need for him to be around.

"It was spent training with my men. I will need

to judge disputes this afternoon, and that is one of the things I hate to do. It takes up a great deal of time, but it is something that is required of me. I used to help my father because he believed I should be trained to take over for him in every way."

"Where do you do the judging?" she asked, having never seen it. Her father had never had a dispute with another that would need to go before the lord.

"Here in the great hall. I only have to do it once a week, for which I am grateful." He rubbed the back of his neck, already dreading the task. He had never done it on his own, and he wished he could ask his father to come and help him. But he was married, which made him the lord of the castle. There would be no more leaning on his father or anyone else.

"May I watch?" There was little for her to do with all the servants about, and she was already wishing for more tasks.

He nodded. "If you would like, I would be honored to have you at my side." Mayhap it would help him to make the right decisions if she was sitting there watching. He wanted to be a better man for Matilda, which was one of the things that told him she was meant to be his bride.

The judging was not like what Matilda had

expected. She had expected there to be great thoughtful judgements, but most of the disputes were ridiculous.

"Milord, my neighbor's pig has gotten into my field three times this week, and he has eaten some of my crops." The peasant who complained had his arms folded over his chest. He glared at the man who stood beside him.

"My pig is getting out because *my neighbor* was not careful and broke the fence around the pig's pen. I have not the tools to fix it, and I have not the time in the middle of the growing season." The neighbor of the first man shook his head. "He should have fixed my fence as he promised the day he broke it."

Robert sat for a moment. "The two of you will work together to fix the fence instead of taking a day of rest tomorrow. Then the animal will no longer be a problem for either of you."

Both men looked unhappy with the solution, but they bowed their heads in agreement and walked toward the entrance to the castle.

Matilda liked the answer, but she wondered why the men could not have come to the same conclusion themselves. Why would they drag their lord into the middle of a silly argument like that? Did not they understand he had a new wife to make love with?

When the judging was finally over and the room was cleared, Matilda looked at Robert for a moment. "You did very well. I think I would have become angry that they could not solve their problems like adults and came to me with such petty disputes."

Robert smiled. "I felt like it at times, but it is the order of things. If I have a dispute with another lord, we will go *together* before the king."

"Have you *met* the king?" she asked.

He nodded. "My father took me to court when I was young. He took us all on different trips, wanting us to see how frivolous things were there so we would not want to become a part of it." His memories of court were not pleasant ones. There had been too many women married to one and flirting with another. Too many men who wanted to stab one another in the back by the looks on their faces. No, he had not been fond of court at all.

"Did it work?"

"I am here and not there. Aye, it worked out well. I think that trip to court told me that I did not *want* to marry a lady. I wanted someone who had real thoughts and real concerns, not someone who complained if her dress was an inch too long or her slippers were not white enough." He shook his head.

"I will remember to never complain about those things, milord."

He laughed. "I think you could complain about anything, and I would not grow angry about it." He grinned at her, stroking her cheek with the back of his fingers. "If you complain, I know it will be about something monumental, like your children not having enough food."

"You should not tell me that . . . what if I become one of those women who does nothing but complain about everything? Would that not make you a little crazy?" Her grin made it clear she was joking with him.

"I am not sure . . . I know my mother had very difficult pregnancies. They were so bad my grandmother would come here and stay with her the entire pregnancy. She did that all seven times. She would have to heal Mother a little every day simply so she could keep food in her stomach. If my father could live through the complaining she must have done to deal with that, then I can make it through any complaining you feel the need to do."

After supper that evening, they went for a walk, the same as they had been taking since the day they had met. "I do love our walks," Matilda said softly as they walked hand-in-hand. The castle was such a beautiful place to live, but at this time of evening, with the sun setting over the trees off in the distance, she believed that she was truly in the most wonderful place God had created on earth.

"I like our walks. I love our time in bed," he said, causing her to blush. He could not help but wonder how long it would be before she wasn't embarrassed by the things he said to her.

"You are not supposed to talk about that!"

"Why not? We are married. We are doing nothing that we are not supposed to do! I need to get my fun in before the babies start coming and keeping me from you . . ."

"You do not want children?" It was the first time Matilda had heard him say anything that would indicate that he did not want all seven of the sons they would someday have to arrive the following day. She thought he was very desperate for those children to be born.

"I do want children. I just want time alone with my new wife first. Time to be together and get to know each other better . . . time to make love . . ." He shrugged. "And as the first male of the family born with power, we are not sure what will happen with our children. The youngest could be like me with powers, or he could simply have the luck that my father always had."

"Do you have a preference?" She was not sure

what she would do if her son was as powerful as her husband. Would she be able to control a child like that?

He shook his head. "Not really. I guess it would be nice to know that my son had the ability to defend himself, but if it does not happen, the world will not end."

She smiled at that, sitting down on what she privately thought of as their kissing bench. "If you could choose any power in the world, what would you want?"

He thought about it for a moment. "I do not know a lot of powers. My great aunt Christiana can talk to people in her mind. My great aunt Eva can make people see things that are not there. My grandmother has the ability to heal with a touch. I guess I am partial to my power, though. It is a part of me, and it feels special. What power would you want?"

"I think I would want to heal with a touch. I cannot imagine wanting any other power. That one could do so much." If she had that power, she could save people from the pain of losing children that her mother had spent years having to deal with. Surely that power would be better than any other.

"I have heard tales of my great-grandfather. He did not like the fact that his daughters had powers, and he made them hide what they could do. He was always afraid they had end up being burned as witches, but it never happened. Everyone who knew them knew they used the power *only* for good."

"That makes sense. I am glad he was not able to stop them. If God gives you a power, you should use it for the good of the world."

"I was named after him."

"You were? Your mother's grandfather?" she asked.

"Aye. He fought in the Battle of Hastings against the Norman army, but he pledged fealty to the man who came in and married his eldest daughter." He made a face. "I wonder if we will have three babes at once. My grandmother has two sisters who were born at the same time she was."

"I hope not! I cannot imagine having even one, let alone three! My mother would be very worried." She shook her head. "Most of her babes were born dead."

"I know it worries you that might happen with us, but it will not. My family always has seven healthy sons. The youngest son has never done anything else." He squeezed her hand. "All of the sons live to adulthood as well. I know it is odd to know our destiny that way, but my family always has."

ROBERT

"I hope it is that way for us." Matilda got to her feet and held her hand out for his. "I think it is time we went to our chamber. Talking about babies makes me want to make one."

Robert grinned. "I cannot argue with that."

"Good. I hate it when you argue . . ."

IT WAS NOT A FULL MONTH LATER WHEN Matilda realized she was expecting. Robert's mother had warned her it would happen quickly, but Matilda had not believed it would be *that* quick. She sat on the edge of her bed one morning after losing the contents of her stomach, wishing she had been able to wait just a little longer. She did not feel like she and Robert had been married long enough for everything to change for them as it would now that she was carrying his babe.

She wanted babes, and she wanted them soon, but they had only had a month together as man and wife. She had just realized she loved her husband, and she had not yet found the right time to tell him how she felt. More importantly, she would have been waiting for those words from him, and they had yet to come.

Every night, he told her he adored her. He cared

for her. He wanted her. But love was never spoken about.

She had gotten into a good routine and was running the castle well. She often sat with her mother and Mary and helped them sew in the afternoons. Enjoying the time of chatting over the needlework had made her transition into the lady of the house much easier.

Matilda was not sure how she was going to tell Robert that she was already expecting. He had made it clear he wanted a little more time alone with her before the children started to come, and she hoped he would not be angry with her. Of course, he had certainly done his share to help make a baby, but that did not matter. She had yet to see him angry, and she did not want this to be the first time.

She wondered if it would be better to wait to say something, let him think they had a little more time to be alone than they really did. Her mother would most certainly be a huge help once the baby was there, but only she could feed her baby, and only she could grow it. No matter how much help she had, her time with Robert would still be limited by a babe.

She was still sitting on the edge of her bed thinking about it a few minutes later when Mary slipped into the room. "I thought I heard you up and about." Mary opened her trunk and chose one of her dresses for her. "This one. I think this is perfect for today." It was a new gown Matilda had yet to wear, and it was in royal purple. Matilda loved the color, and she wanted to wear it. Soon it would need to be let out in the waist.

"Aye, let us wear that one." Matilda stood, removing her nightgown so Mary could help her into the beautiful new dress. "I think this is going to be my favorite."

"You say that with every new gown we make," Mary said with a laugh. "It is nice to know you appreciate the work we do."

"I am so glad you and Mama are getting along so well. It feels right that you are making my dresses together." And soon, the three of them could work together during the long winter to make clothes for the babe.

"I am so glad she is here. She is made my job so much easier, and I simply enjoy being around her."

"My mother is your mother," Matilda said with a smile, turning around after her dress was fastened in the back. "Thank you, Mary. I think I am going to go for a walk today. I have need to spend some time alone." Not that she would truly be alone with Robert's babe growing within her.

Mary frowned. "I will walk with you. I am not

sure how Lord Robert would feel about you wandering off the grounds by yourself."

"I will be fine. Thank you, Mary." With those words, Matilda headed down the stairs and toward the woods near the castle. Time alone was exactly what she needed.

CHAPTER NINE

As soon as Matilda stepped into the woods, she wondered if she was making a mistake. As well-loved as Robert's family was, she was simply a new bride, and she might not have the protection his family afforded him.

She decided after a moment that she was being silly and continued her walk, thinking about what she would do about the babe she carried. She knew she had to tell Robert, but should she tell him now or wait a month or two until she was showing before she said something? She wanted him to have as long with just the two of them as she could give him. As soon as she announced the baby, they would begin preparing for a time when they were no longer alone. Their family would be three and not two.

The woods were dark considering how bright the sun was shining that afternoon, and she walked along, completely lost in thought. She had to figure out when to talk to Robert. She was very excited about carrying his first son, but she wanted him to be just as excited when she told him. What if he was disappointed that she had conceived so soon? She was not sure if she could bear it.

Just as she was about to step out into the sunshine on the other side of the wooded area, she noticed two men, who appeared to be nobleman, walking together. They both carried swords and looked intent on doing some mischief. They were young, not much older than she was herself, and she knew she was tempting fate by continuing on the way she was, so she turned to head back the other way.

She had only gone a few steps when she heard the branches crushing rapidly behind her, so she took off in a run, screaming as loudly as she could. If the men were intent on hurting her, they would do so before anyone could reach them, but screaming seemed to be her only protection.

A hand grabbed her upper arm and spun her around to face them. "Please, let me go. My husband is the lord here, and he will not be happy if you harm me." She could see on the stranger's face that her pleas were for naught, but she had to try. The babe she carried needed to be protected!

The two men were both dark-haired and angry looking. "Your husband never has to know what you do with us," the man holding her arm said, leaning down over her. His mouth pressed against her neck, and she felt chills run through her.

Once again, she screamed as loudly as she could as the man backed her against one of the trees. She tried to throw him away from her, hating that he pressed his body against hers in a way that only a married man should do with his wife.

The other man was licking his lips and watching with an amused look on his face. Matilda turned her head away, kicking at the man holding her as hard as she could, her screams still filling the air.

Suddenly there was nothing for her to fight against. The man who had been pressing her into the tree flew through the air away from her as if a giant hand had struck him away from her. She leaned back against the tree, her hand covering her mouth to stop the screams that wanted to keep going on forever.

As she watched, the man who had been holding her rolled to his hands and knees to get back on his feet, and his sword came out of his scabbard, plunging into his back, a pool of blood forming on the leaves below him.

The other man backed up a few feet, staring behind her, and he turned and ran away, leaving his friend lying on the wooded ground in a heap, his own sword plunged through his back.

Matilda held back a sob as she covered her face with her hands. Even though the men did not know what had happened, she did. Her husband, her sweet, gentle Robert, had used his powers to save her—and to kill a nobleman. It was her fault, and she hated that he had been pressed to commit murder on her behalf.

A moment later, Robert was in front of her, his arms around her, holding her close. "Did they hurt you?"

Matilda shook her head. She would have some bruises the next day, but her injuries were nothing compared to the man who had attacked her so savagely. He was obviously dead just feet away from them, and another nobleman had watched it all unfold.

"Robert, he had a friend with him who was watching. You were seen killing a nobleman."

"My wife was attacked by the nobleman I killed. I promise you the king would have dispatched anyone who had touched his wife in the same manner, and he will only have good things to say about what I have done here." And truthfully, he did not care what the king said. His family had left many countries in its history, and he was willing to leave this one if it meant having her safe.

She could not believe his nonchalant attitude about the whole thing. "But . . . what if people say you are a witch? That your powers come from Satan? Are you not worried that you will be burned?"

He shook his head. "No one would dare say something like that against my family. I do not know these men, but I do know they were trespassing on my property, and they were trying to harm my wife. They will never have the chance again."

She started to argue with him but found herself swept up in his arms and carried back through the woods toward the castle. "Put me down, Robert! You will hurt yourself carrying me so far!"

"You weigh no more than a child, Matilda. I do not know how you are going to be strong enough to carry my babe!" But there was no doubt in his mind she would be. Never had a woman in his lineage lost her life in childbirth. They all lived to see their seven sons grow old.

Matilda remained silent. She knew it was the right time to tell him about the baby she carried, but after what had just happened . . . she needed some time to calm down first. "Where are you taking me?"

"To the castle to your mother and Mary. I do not want you leaving alone again. You need to have one of my men with you at all times." He shook his head. "I cannot believe we have never discussed this before. As a serf, you were able to go where you wanted and do what you would, but as a lady, you need to stay close to safety. I will not have you hurt."

Matilda sighed. "I like being free to go where I will. Do you really think I need someone with me? After what just happened, I fear no one will ever be willing to come on your land again. They will all think that pagans dwell in those woods, ready to kill anyone who trespasses."

"I hope they do! I will not allow a man to touch you!"

She shuddered as she thought about the dead man lying in the woods. "What about the . . ."

"The man who attacked you? His body will be dealt with."

She buried her face in his neck. "I hate that I was the reason you killed an equal . . ."

"No man who would attack a woman the way that man did is an equal. He is a disgusting, evil man who needed to be killed. I did the entire land of England a favor by taking his life. And I certainly did him a favor by doing it quickly. I would have liked to have seen him suffer."

They reached the castle, and he waited as one of his men hurried forward and opened the door for him before striding up the stairs with her still in his arms. He went to the room where her mother sewed with Mary and set her on her feet, opening the door and guiding her inside.

Quickly he explained what had happened. "Please watch her and do not let her leave. I am about to go fetch my mother to examine her and make sure nothing is amiss. Then I am going to have someone dispose of the body in my woods." Robert did not wait for anyone to agree with what he had said. Instead he left the room and went in search of some men to deal with the body.

Once that task was completed, he strode to his mother's house, anger filling him. He was angry with Matilda because she had left the castle which was protected to go for a walk in the woods. He had never told her to not go there, but she should have had the sense to know it was not safe!

Mostly, though, he was angry with the man who had dared to touch his wife. She was his, and no one had the right to even look at her unless he gave his permission. Whether she had once been a serf or not, she belonged to him and therefore had his full protection behind her. It would be known throughout the kingdom that to touch his wife meant death.

When he reached his parents' house, he pounded on the door and waited for a servant to come bid him entry. Instead his mother opened the door. "Robert, what is wrong with you?"

He had barely begun his explanation when she put her hand over her mouth in shock. "I will get my bag."

He waited, pacing back and forth in front of the house, as his mother got her healing bag, which held all her potions and herbs she used to help others.

As soon as she was there, the two of them walked quickly back toward the castle, with him finishing the story as they walked. "She said she was not hurt, but I do not see how she could not have been. There must be some bruises. I want them gone."

His mother nodded. "I have potions that will make bruises fade much quicker than normal. I will see to it." She had never seen her son so angry. "Has someone dealt with the body?" she asked softly.

"I sent three men to take care of it." A stick in front of them floated into the air before snapping in half, showing just how angry he was. "I have never in my life felt this kind of anger, Mother. That man had his hands on Matilda."

"I know, Robert. I will make sure she is all right. You need to stay in the castle until your anger is gone. You do not want to risk exposing your powers to anyone outside of our family. You have already done that once today, and if it continues, we will have problems. We both know our powers come from God, but others believe that anyone with the kind of powers we have are pagans. We must be careful."

He nodded, opening the door to the castle for her and climbing the stairs two at a time. When he reached the room where he had left his wife, he found her sitting on the side of the bed, Mary on one side of her and Esther on the other.

His mother pushed him out of the way and went to Matilda. "Let us go to your chamber so I can examine you. All right?"

Matilda nodded. She did not care what happened to her anymore. Nothing was right with the world. She did not know if it ever would be again. A man she did not know had put his hands on her, and his intentions had been clear. He had planned to take something from her that she had given to her husband and him alone.

In her room, her mother-in-law bid her undress, so she could look at the wounds made. After her dress was unfastened, she dropped it to her feet, sitting in just her shift on the edge of her bed.

Lady Lina looked at the bruise forming on her wrist and quickly added an ointment. "You are not going to be able to keep Robert from seeing this, but the salve will stop the bruise from getting too dark." She looked at Matilda, studying her closely. "They did not hurt you?"

"No more than what you see." Matilda frowned. "I do worry they may have harmed the babe, though."

Lady Lina's eyes widened. "The babe?" She looked both excited and horrified. "Have you noticed blood?"

Matilda shook her head. "I do think I am all right, but I just realized I carried this morning. I was walking and thinking about how much my life has changed, and I was attacked."

"I am going to give you a potion for if you have trouble keeping food down and another to build your strength. I want you taking them both every morning. All right?"

"Aye. I will take them."

Lady Lina bit her lip and got to her feet. "I think I want my mother to come and make sure all is well with you. Do you mind if I send for her?"

Matilda frowned. "Do you think it is necessary?"

"I do not know, but I would feel much better if she was here. It will take her three days to make the journey once she receives my message. She is old now and cannot travel as quickly as she once could."

"Send for her. We do not want to risk the babe."

"Thank you." Lady Lina smiled at Matilda and squeezed her hand. "It is just a precaution. I am sure that babe will be as strong as all seven of my sons were." With those words, she strode from the room, closing the door behind her. She went to Mary first, asking her to help Matilda dress, and then she went to Robert.

"How is she?"

"She has a bruise forming on her wrist, but there are no other real injuries that I can see. I am going to send for my mother to examine her, but that is just a precaution. I cannot risk your son being hurt. If he is, Mother can heal him."

"My son?"

Lady Lina covered her mouth with her hand. "I assumed she had told you! Please do not tell her you know. She should be the one who tells you that you will be a father. She just realized this morning, so I am sure it is just a matter of time until she has a chance."

He nodded, shocked to his core. His wife was attacked, he killed in revenge, and found out he was to be a father all in one day. It was a bit more than he was used to handling all at once. "I am going to go see her. I do not want to let her out of my sight until Grandmother comes. I need to be sure she is all right."

"That sounds good to me. If she starts to bleed, you will need to send for me right away." His mother was halfway out the door before she paused and turned back to him. "Your father and I are going to ride to where we can talk to Aunt Christiana. We will come for supper tonight, so we can all be together, and I will be close if there is a problem."

Robert stared at the spot where his mother had been long after she was gone. He was thankful to have her to help him, but he worried about the future of his family. If he continued to get as angry as he had that morning, there would be no way he could hide his powers.

By the time his grandmother arrived three days later, Robert was angry with Matilda. She had yet to tell him about the babe she carried, and he wondered if she ever planned to tell him. He knew she was distracted by the attack, but it had been days. She had told his mother she was expecting, so why not him?

His grandparents came to the castle, both of them ready to see him. His grandfather hugged him close. "Hello, Grandfather. Thank you for coming."

His grandmother did not waste time with pleasantries. She headed straight up the stairs to the master bedchamber and knocked.

Matilda was lying on her side, feeling nauseated when a knock came to the door. "Aye?"

The door opened, and an elderly woman she had never seen before entered the room and walked over to sit on the bed beside her. "I am Marina, Lina's mother. How are you feeling?"

The question from a stranger had Matilda sobbing. "I worry about the babe!"

"Of course you do. I have never known a woman who was carrying her first child who did not worry about the babe inside her. May I have your permission to check you?"

Matilda nodded, brushing away a tear. "Should I sit?"

Marina shook her head. "It does not matter, child. I can help you no matter how you lay." Her hand hovered over Matilda's abdomen, and she smiled. "The babe is strong. There is no problem at all." After another moment, she said, "I have healed your wrist. It was a little worse than I was led to believe." Then she made a face. "You are having trouble keeping food in you."

Matilda struggled to sit up. "I am having trouble with food, but I am getting some to stay in me. Usually I only miss out on the morning meal completely."

"Do you mind if I heal you a little bit so you can eat more?"

"Not at all. It would be nice not to share my meal with the chamber pot every morning."

Marina laughed. "My daughter has told me many good things about you. She says you make Robert a very happy man. I thank you for that."

Matilda bit her lip, studying the older woman. "You know I was a serf?" she asked.

"Nay, that has never come up. It does not matter anyway. You are my new granddaughter whether you were born a serf or a princess."

"This family never ceases to amaze me. You are all so warm and welcoming. I think I could tell you that I was a druid who was hatched from an egg in a forest in Scotland, and you would not even blink."

"I am afraid I would. A Scotswoman as a granddaughter? I draw the line there!"

Matilda laughed, feeling her nausea abate as

Marina held her hand over her abdomen. "I feel better already."

"I am going to stay here for a few days. By the time I leave, we will have your morning sickness under control. It is not bad." Marina reached out and helped Matilda to her feet. "Now, let us go downstairs, so we can all chat. My husband is here with me, and we have both been very curious about the new granddaughter we have."

Matilda was surprised at just how spry Robert's grandmother was. "What should I call you?"

"I would love it if you called us Grandmama and Grandfather like Robert does."

Matilda nodded. "I would like that." She took the stairs slowly and went into the parlor where she had first met Robert, sitting on the window seat there with her husband, while the others took chairs around the house. "Robert, have you let your parents know that your grandparents are here yet?"

Robert shook his head. "I guess I should do that, should I not?" He gave her a sad look as he left, and she could not imagine what was wrong with him.

Marina looked at Matilda. "He does not seem as happy as I expected him to be. He is married, and his first son is on the way. What reason does he have for sadness?"

Matilda shook her head. "I have not told him

about the babe yet. I just found out the day of my attack, and I have not been sure quite how to broach the subject. I know he wants to wait a little while before having children."

"That explains his unhappiness then. Do you really think he does not know? And you keeping it from him will upset him because he *does* know."

"How *could* he know?"

Marina shook her head at Matilda. "There is something about the Lain women when they are carrying. Their faces glow . . . it is hard to explain, but even if I had not known you were expecting upon my arrival, I would have known when I saw your face. He knows you are hiding it from him."

Matilda bit her lip. "I suppose it is time to tell him then, is not it?"

"Not only time to tell him, but time to tell him why you have tried to hide something so very obvious from him. I know my grandson well enough to know he is very bothered by the deception." Marina smiled then. "Let me introduce you to your new grandfather while we wait. This is Charles Nobilis, the Norman who came onto our land and conquered my heart many years ago."

"It is nice to meet you, sir."

CHAPTER TEN

Through the long afternoon with Robert's family, Matilda noticed that Robert looked sad all the time. His grandmother was right, and she definitely needed to tell him that she was carrying. But how could she explain why she had not yet told him?

Supper that evening was a boisterous meal including Matilda's parents as well as Robert's parents and grandparents. After the meal, Matilda slipped her hand into Robert's. "Let us walk."

He nodded, not looking directly at her. "We can walk, but it is raining outside."

Lady Lina shook her head. "As if your mother cannot fix that." She stepped outside with them and waved her arms, stopping the rain immediately. "I will have it start raining again when you come back in. The farmers have complained there is been too little rain this year."

Matilda thanked her sweetly for her intervention, and the young couple began their walk. "I owe you an apology, Robert," Matilda finally said when it was obvious Robert was not going to say anything.

"Oh?" Robert asked. "And why is that?"

"Because I did not tell you as soon as I knew I was expecting. I could lie and say that I forgot about it as soon as I was attacked in the woods, but it would be just that. A lie. I did not forget at all, and all I could think about was that the babe might have been injured." She shook her head. "But that is not why I did not tell you." She hated that she had to confess all of this, but she knew if she did not, they would never have peace between them.

He frowned, looking at her as if she had lost her mind. "Then why did not you tell me?"

"I had already decided not to tell you. I wanted to wait a little longer. I wanted our marriage to be just about the two of us. When we talked about having babies right after we married, you made me feel like you would like to wait a little while. I must have conceived this babe on our wedding night or the night after." She sighed. "Your grandmother says the babe is growing well, and that she is going to stay for a few days to heal me. I should be fine before she goes." They had reached the kissing bench, so she sat down.

Robert sat beside her, looking at her with concern. "Why does she need to heal you?"

Matilda shrugged. "I do not think she really does *need* to heal me, but she wants to. I have some morning sickness, and she would like for me to be able to keep more meals inside me. It is not anything close to as bad as what your mother went through, from what I am told."

"I wish you had told me. I did want some time alone with you before the babies started coming, but in my family, we seem to get that time after all our sons are raised and not a minute before." He shook his head. "Of course, I want the babe you are carrying and all the others that will come. Please do not hide things from me again."

She frowned, looking down at her hands. "I guess there is something else I have been hiding too. I did not mean to hide it, but . . ." If she was confessing to her deceptions, she may as well confess to all at once and not save some for later.

Robert felt himself getting angry. How could they have a good marriage if she was not completely honest with him? "What are you hiding?"

When Matilda looked up, she could see a rock

floating in the air, and she had no doubt how it got there. "I am sorry to anger you, Robert. I did not mean to."

He saw the rock floating, and he forced himself to breathe slowly and lowered it. "What else have you been hiding?" He took her hand and held it. "I will try not to get angry."

"It is not really something as important as expecting a baby . . ." He owned her body, but she had kept him from knowing about her love because she had felt that was one thing he could not command. He could not make her love him, so she had avoided telling him. "I love you, Robert. I have loved you for a while now."

"Is that what you were hiding?" His heart started beating faster, and he turned to her completely.

"Aye, that is the only thing. I promise." She hoped that would not anger him.

He pulled her onto his lap with the hand he was holding, enveloping her in his arms. "Do you have any idea how long I have waited for you to say those words?"

"As long as I have been waiting for you to say them, I would imagine." She looked into his eyes, wondering if she would ever hear him tell her he loved her. He was a strong man, and she was not sure how often they admitted to loving their wives.

"You think I would have wanted to marry you if I did not love you? My love came fast. I heard you talking about me, I saw you dusting, and my heart was yours. I all but followed you around like a lost dog, and you still did not seem to share my feelings." He pulled her down for a long kiss. "There is never been a woman that I could imagine spending my life with before you. Now that we are married, I am never letting you go. Do you understand what that means?"

She smiled at him, still a little confused by what he was saying. Did he love her or did not he?

"I love you more than I ever imagined I would be able to love. You are mine, Matilda Lain, until death do us part." He kissed her again, wishing they were already in their chamber so they could become one. "God blessed me the day you came into my life."

"Nay, He blessed me!"

"He blessed us." Robert stood and led her into the castle and up to their bedchamber. She was the woman he loved above all others, and he would happily prove it to her once again.

EPILOGUE

1146

Matilda no longer noticed that guards that always accompanied her on her walks into the woods. Her mother went along, because with seven boys in tow, one was bound to get into mischief.

Robert's guards did their best to blend into the background, so the children were rarely aware of their presence, which pleased Matilda. She did not want her sons to know that their world was a dangerous and dark place. Not yet anyway.

Her youngest, Braden, seemed to have no powers, and Matilda was not yet sure if she was happy or sad about it. Robert was an aberration in his family, and the powers would end with him. He still amused her by moving things about with his mind at times, but he was much more careful about letting the powers show to outsiders.

Braden was looking all around at the ground for something, and Matilda crouched down beside him, happy to have her youthful figure back and be able to squat as the boy was. "What are we looking for?" she asked softly.

At only three summers old, Braden was full of mischief and kept her and her mother on their toes constantly. "I want to pick a flower for my mama."

Matilda smiled, feeling a pang. It was late fall, and there would be no more weeds brought to her and called flowers for several months. "It is almost winter, Braden. We will not have flowers again until the spring, but then I would love for you to pick me a whole armful of flowers." Having little boys bring her flowers had to be one of her very favorite parts of being a mother of sons.

"The flowers are there. Just under the dirt. Cannot you feel them, Mama?" He placed his small hand on the leaves on the forest floor and stared at it expectantly. When nothing happened, he frowned and moved the leaves out of the way, so he could touch the ground. "Grow!"

Matilda grinned as she watched her son looking

at the earth expectantly. His imagination was so active and good. She loved all of her children equally of course, but this youngest one—this one who thought he could make flowers grow at will. He made her smile just a bit more than the others.

She was so busy watching Braden that she almost missed it. Several flowers grew before her eyes, popping out of the earth. Braden clapped his little hands together before plucking each of them and making a small bouquet to present to his mother. "Here, Mama. I knew the flowers were there. I just had to tell them to grow!"

Matilda took the flowers she had been presented with, her eyes meeting her mother's over the top of the boy's head. Her mother had long been apprised of the powers her husband's family tended to have, but neither of them had expected it in little Braden. "Thank you, Braden. The flowers are beautiful."

"I think I am going to grow flowers when I grow up. Can I be a gardener instead of a knight?"

Her oldest son, Alex, who was named after his grandfather, laughed. "Braden, you *have* to be a knight. Someday the castle is going to be yours, and you cannot run around growing flowers instead of brandishing a sword!" Already Alex carried a wooden sword and challenged her second son, James, to fights often.

James pulled out his sword, and the two boys began sword fighting there in the woods, unaware of the miracle they had just experienced. Braden had the power to grow flowers from a barren earth.

Matilda hugged Braden to her. "I think you should grow all the flowers you want to grow. You are truly special, my son."

Braden squirmed away, wanting to go stand with his brothers to watch the two oldest fight. He had already forgotten about the flowers he had given to his mother, but she had not. How could she? Her son was powerful . . . just like his father.

ABOUT THE AUTHOR

kirstenandmorganna.com

ALSO BY KIRSTEN OSBOURNE

If you enjoyed this book and would like to receive emails when Kirsten has new books out, please text 'Bob' to 42828.

For a complete list of Kirsten's works head to her website wwww.kirstenandmorganna.com

Made in the
USA
Columbia, SC